'Don't like me very much, do you, Sister?' Duncan said mockingly. 'No one must say a word against the golden boy of the CU, is that it? Well, too bad if you won't face facts but he's a drunk and I'll shout it from the rooftops if it will protect his patients!'

'He's not a drunk,' Jennet refuted stonily, sick with hurt and dismay as the blunt words assailed her ears. 'He's had a bad time lately, that's all.'

'He lost his wife in a road accident. I know about that.' It was impatient.

'Everyone knows—but other people understand, make allowances . . .'

'Cover up for his mistakes, you mean! Well, I'm not prepared to do so when lives may be at stake, Sister,' he informed her bluntly. 'Maybe it isn't ethical to speak out against my boss but I'm not going to let him carve up patients like an incompetent because he's been hitting the bottle half the night and can't keep his hand from shaking!'

Lynne Collins has written twenty-five Medical Romances based on personal experience of hospital life backed by research and information from her many friends in the medical profession. She likes writing about hospital settings, with their wealth of human interest. Married with one son and now living on the Essex coast, Lynne enjoys travel, meeting people, talking, walking and gardening. She has also written several Medical Romances under the pen-name of Lindsay Hicks.

Previous Titles

STAR SURGEON
SURGEON AT BAY

BEAT OF THE HEART

BY

LYNNE COLLINS

MILLS & BOON LIMITED
ETON HOUSE   18-24 PARADISE ROAD
RICHMOND   SURREY   TW9 1SR

First published in Great Britain 1989 by Mills & Boon Limited

© Lynne Collins 1989

Australian copyright 1989 Philippine copyright 1989 This edition 1989

ISBN 0 263 76641 1

Set in Times 11 on 11½ pt. 03 – 8911 – 55300

Typeset in Great Britain by JCL Graphics, Bristol

Made and Printed in Great Britain

CHAPTER ONE

IT WAS hotter than Athens in August in the operating theatre that morning! Conscious of the slow, irritating trickle of perspiration between her breasts beneath the figure-disguising green gown, Jennet sighed and wished that she was still sunning herself on the beach of a Greek island.

Usually, she couldn't wait to get back to the job she loved after a holiday, but it seemed that the Fitzroy Foundation Hospital and its busy theatres had lost some of their charm for her at last. No doubt those blissful days—and nights—with Jeff were responsible for that . . .

Jennet thrust the thought of the attractive American from mind as she checked the array of surgical instruments with a comprehensive glance and then covered them with a sterile drape. She would probably never see him again, she told herself sensibly. Holiday romances were notorious for fading away—and perhaps that was a good thing. She had said and done things in the heat of the moment and the Greek sunshine that she might blush to recall if she ever met Jeff again beneath England's often overcast skies!

In the adjoining scrub annexe, the surgical team were preparing for the first procedure and she could hear the buzz of talk, the occasional shout of male laughter. As a department, Theatres was friendly, informal, a pleasant place to work in spite of the demands and pressures of surgery. Jennet had been a theatre sister for eighteen months and had no wish to return to ward work.

Suddenly, a voice that she didn't recognise cut across another man's words. 'I don't deny that Carter has a splendid reputation behind him. It's his future that seems to be in doubt! Let's hope he can get through today's list without losing some poor devil on the table—if he turns up at all! The man's a menace to his patients and a liability to the rest of us, in my opinion!'

It wasn't the attractive timbre in the deep voice that snatched Jennet's attention but the words uttered in a strongly critical tone. She turned to look at the speaker, swift anger sparking.

At least six feet two, he had the shoulders of a rugger player, bronzed good looks and the confident air of a man who knew what he wanted and how to get it. Impressive, she had thought earlier, glancing at him more than once as she went about her work, struck by his height and powerful build. Now, she put out a hand to detain a passing nurse.

'Who *is* that man?' she demanded coldly.

Holly Mason followed the direction of the theatre sister's irate gaze. 'Duncan Blair, the new registrar,' she obliged. 'Haven't you met him yet? Tasty, isn't he? He's caused quite a stir among the first-years, I believe!' Smiling, the staff nurse hurried away.

Jennet's mouth tightened as she continued to study the surgeon with hard eyes. Busy with the usual rush of getting Theatre Three ready, she had forgotten about the man who had taken up his appointment in the Cardiac Unit while she was on holiday. He was said to be clever and dedicated, a valuable addition to Paul Carter's team. He was also a man who didn't mince his words, apparently—or care who happened to be listening!

In other circumstances Jennet might have admired someone who wasn't afraid to speak his mind. But that slur on a senior and much superior surgeon was not only unethical but unforgivable in her eyes!

As he struggled to adjust his gown over broad shoulders, he became aware of her disapproving scrutiny. Their eyes met, and Jennet saw a flicker of surprise and then a spark of answering antagonism in his grey gaze before he turned, with a dismissive shrug, to the junior nurse who sped to tie his strings.

Seeing the girl's fluttering reaction to the charm of a slightly crooked smile, Jennet was unreasonably irritated. 'I need you here, Nurse Moore!' she called sharply. 'I'm sure Mr Blair can manage to tie his own strings!'

The nurse hurried to respond to the note of authority in the theatre sister's call, throwing a smile over her shoulder at the registrar. Jennet saw a glint of sardonic amusement in Duncan Blair's eyes, but she was responsible for the running of the theatre and she had no intention of allowing its efficiency to be undermined by a good-looking newcomer.

Later, as she was standing tense and poised to assist the consultant, waiting for the anaesthetist to complete the careful check of dials and monitors, her glance travelled idly over the gowned and masked figures of the assembled team and came to a halt at the easily identifiable newcomer.

He turned his proud head to capture her gaze,

steely grey eyes intent but impossible to read. Jennet felt foolishly embarrassed, however, to be caught staring by the man whose arrival had apparently caused a minor sensation among the junior nurses. She had no desire to be lumped with the first-years who took a flirtatious interest in every male addition to the hospital staff.

Fair-skinned, she blushed much too easily and hated it. Now, feeling the glow in her face, she was grateful for the mask that covered nose and mouth and hot cheeks. But, before the registrar's continued, cool assessment, the tide of warm colour crept to the roots of thick blonde hair bundled into her mob cap and she saw sudden, scornful impatience leap into those riveting eyes.

Thick, gold-tipped lashes instantly dropped to veil her annoyance at that summary dismissal of her as just another impressionable female. Jennet smarted at the snubbing rejection in the narrowed eyes. Was he so pursued and so flattered by women that he automatically assumed an unwelcome admiration in her interest? Damn his arrogance! She felt a stir of defensive dislike to add to her disapproval of Duncan Blair.

The anaesthetist gave the nod for by-pass surgery to proceed. 'All set, sir . . .'

Paul Carter turned to the slender theatre sister at his side. 'Quite ready, Sister?' It was routine courtesy, accompanied by a smile reflected in the consultant's warm dark eyes.

Jennet made last-minute checks of instruments and readiness of nurses and nodded. 'Everything seems to be in order, Mr Carter,' she assured him, just as formally, and slapped a scalpel into his outstretched hand. Somehow, it slipped through his fingers to hit the floor with a clatter. 'Sorry,' she said quickly, reaching for a replacement as a dirty nurse darted forward to pick up the offending instrument.

'Entirely my fault, Sister . . .'

Seeing the remorse in his eyes and the brace of his shoulders, Jennet sent him an understanding, affectionate glance as she handed him the fresh scalpel. Grasping it firmly, he bent over his patient and made the first incision. It was a trifle clumsy, she thought in dismay, troubled by the deterioration in his skills in the few weeks that she had been away. He didn't look well that morning, either. He was pale and strained and already beads of sweat stood out on his handsome brow, she realised, concerned.

Another bad night, perhaps . . .?

Tension mounted as the consultant worked with surprising slowness and an unusual lack of dexterity to prepare the patient for the insertion of a by-pass artery. Eyes exchanged wary glances above masks. Duncan Blair ventured to suggest an alternative approach and was snubbed with a smiling rejection from an invariably courteous but determined senior surgeon. Ben Drummond, the anaesthetist, became even more intent on monitoring the unconscious patient on the table and it was obvious to Jennet's experienced eyes that things were not going well.

No one dared to say so, however. It wasn't ethical to question or challenge a surgeon of his standing. But he couldn't be unaware of the growing unease, Jennet thought heavily, sensing his inner struggle with the doubts and apprehension that eroded his ability.

Suddenly he threw an artery clamp into a receiver and turned from the operating-table. 'Take over here, Blair. I don't feel too good,' he said brusquely and strode from the theatre, tearing at his mask with an impatient hand.

An audible sigh of relief rippled round the room. Jennet's heart sank. Having watched the betraying tremble of those clever hands, the too frequent hesitations, and observed the growing lack of confidence, she felt that he had acted wisely in handing over to his registrar. No surgeon could afford to take chances—and certainly not one as renowned and respected as Paul Carter with his international reputation as a courageous and forward-looking cardiac surgeon.

It hurt that he seemed to be accepting the steady deterioration of his skill instead of fighting with all his might against the cause. Looking over her shoulder into the scrub annexe, Jennet saw the surreptitious lift of hand to mouth and her heart sank even further as she realised how much he needed that quick, furtive swallow from the hip-flask that he had begun to carry about with him. It had happened before and worried her then. Now she wondered if it was happening more than she knew and if others had noticed his growing reliance on alcohol.

Duncan Blair, for instance.

Paul would deny that he had a drink problem, of course. His handsome face would light up with his swift, disarming smile and he would put an arm about her shoulders and declare that she was too imaginative, over-anxious. But she would see the shadow behind the smile that the passing months did nothing to diminish, and continue to worry.

Jennet understood the desolation that drove him
to drink too much but she was terribly afraid that
the habit might already have a hold on him that
threatened his work and his health as well as her
peace of mind.

'Best thing he could have done,' Ben Drummond
murmured with a rueful shake of his capped head
as he adjusted the anaesthetic drip, speaking as a
friend.

'He's certainly got the shakes badly this morn ...
ouch!' The tactless junior surgeon turned a
reproachful gaze on the staff nurse who had kicked
him before he realised the fierce glower in Jennet's
amber eyes and subsided, feeling and looking
uncomfortable.

Duncan moved into position at the side of the
stiffly silent theatre sister. 'This is getting to be a
habit,' he said drily. 'Let's see what can be done to
repair the damage this time. Carver might be an
apter name than Carter!'

Jennet looked at him with acute dislike, making
no attempt to pass the instrument that his
peremptorily outstretched hand was demanding.
How dared he criticise a man whose work would
be remembered and revered long after this
newcomer was gone and forgotten! How dared he
sneer at a senior surgeon in front of her nurses and
encourage idiots like Tim Gowan to do the same!
If that was the kind of behaviour she could expect
from the new registrar, then sparks would certainly
fly in the coming weeks!

'When you're quite ready, Sister!'

The snap of the words set her bristling and she
shot a quelling glance at the sardonic surgeon. 'One
moment, Mr Blair,' she said crisply and with an

authority that his attitude threatened to undermine. 'I'm concerned about Mr Carter. He doesn't appear to be well.' She moved slightly for a better view of the annexe but there was now no sign of the consultant.

'I expect he can take perfectly good care of himself, Sister. Right now, the patient is more in need of your concern.' The critical gleam in grey eyes implied disapproval of a surgeon who abruptly abandoned his post and of the theatre sister who was quivering in defensive support.

Without another word, Jennet slapped the scalpel into his palm with almost offensive efficiency, convinced that Theatres wasn't going to be a happier place for Duncan Blair's arrival. She didn't like his arrogant attitude at all!

But, assisting him as he carried out the delicate by-pass surgery, she had to admit that he knew his job, for strong, sure hands cut and clamped and probed and sutured with the skilled economy of movement that was the hallmark of a fine surgeon.

Jennet was so absorbed in playing her own part in the procedure that it seemed very little time before the patient was being wheeled away to the recovery room. Yet she ached all over from the tension of trying to please a man she couldn't like who seemed to demand the very best of her ability as an instrument nurse.

As soon as she had set nurses to clean the operating-room and sterilise the used instruments, she followed the surgeons into the annexe. Most of the team had melted away to change or to enjoy a welcome break in the surgeons' sitting-room before the next procedure. Duncan Blair seemed to be in no hurry to do either.

He tossed his stained gown into the bin as she entered. His thin green tunic clung to him damply, the deep V-neck exposing curling golden hair on a powerful chest. Muscles rippled in the strong shoulders and bare arms as he pulled off his cap and ran a hand through the damp-darkened chestnut waves of thick springy hair that was worn a little long and inclined to curl on the nape of his neck.

Very tall, broad-shouldered and lean-hipped and arrogantly good-looking, he was magnificently male, Jennet admitted dispassionately, wondering how many of the junior nurses were already sighing over the new registrar.

Sending her an indifferent glance, he bent over a basin to sluice cold water over face and head. He wasn't exactly handsome, Jennet decided critically. His nose had been broken at some time, possibly playing rugger in his medical student days, and his mouth with its grim set looked as if it wasn't used to smiling. In fact, the harshness of his rugged features and the coldness of the deep-set grey eyes chilled her as she studied him.

An odd premonitory shiver rippled down her spine as the surgeon abruptly raised his head to look directly into her unguarded eyes. In that moment, Jennet knew in her bones that Duncan Blair was going to be trouble with a capital T . . . 'Think you'll know me again, Sister?' Duncan Blair reached for a towel that obscured an amused glint in his eyes as he rubbed briskly at his wet hair.

Jennet looked away, discomfited. 'Was I staring? Sorry,' she said briskly, seething with fresh dislike. 'I was thinking of something else . . .'

'Still worrying about Carter? No need, Sister.

Wherever he went, he came back in time to watch the end of the performance from the viewing gallery. Nice of him to take an interest in his patient, don't you think?'

Jennet ignored the sardonic jibe. Turning away, she took off her own gown and cap and shook out her hair. The heavy mass tumbled about her shoulders in a shimmering cascade and she swept golden curls back from a face that was small and oval and pretty, grave in repose but lighting to a real and remembered beauty when her warm smile was reflected in striking amber eyes.

Suddenly self-conscious in the thin theatre frock that emphasised narrow waist and small breasts and gently rounded hips, she felt that she was being studied with openly male appreciation and resentment stirred. It wasn't the first time that she had wished to be admired more for her nursing ability than for a face and figure she couldn't help but which had always attracted more attention than she liked, however.

Petite, blonde and eye-catchingly pretty in the famous Fitz uniform with its longer skirt and puffed sleeves, pleated bodice narrowing at the waist, tiny cap almost lost among her shining curls, Jennet had been caused problems by her looks in her first-year days when she'd had to work twice as hard as the rest of her set to convince doubting tutors and suspicious ward sisters that she really wanted to nurse and wasn't merely hoping to find a husband among the young doctors and medical students who swarmed about her.

Now, having done her best for some hours to impress him with her efficiency, she wasn't pleased or flattered to realise that the admiring speculation in Duncan Blair's study had nothing to do with her ability as a theatre sister.

Before she could frame a suitable put-down, Paul strolled in, cheerful and relaxed. 'I couldn't rush off without congratulating you on a splendid performance, Duncan. Well done!' He put a hand on Jennet's shoulder and left it there for a smiling moment. 'This young lady doesn't like me to say so, but you couldn't have had a better scrub nurse. She knows more about cardiac procedures than many surgeons.'

Jennet was embarrassed. It was unlike him to applaud her so openly and she wondered just how much whisky he had got through while his new registrar operated in his place. She frowned at Paul in silent reproach and he grinned back, unrepentant.

The boyish smile made him seem younger than his years but few people believed that he could be forty-four, in spite of the silver wings to his dark hair and the network of tiny lines about his dark eyes. He was a very handsome man, tall and lean and good-looking with a charismatic degree of charm that could still flutter hearts. Jennet loved him very much.

'I hope you're feeling better,' she ventured, knowing his dislike of 'fussing'.

'I'm fine. It's nothing that an hour or two on the golf-course won't cure,' he assured her blithely. He turned to his scowling registrar. 'You're such an excellent deputy that I know I can rely on you to take my clinic and the afternoon round.' It was warmly confident.

'Why not? I've seen more of your patients that you have in the last few weeks.'

It was so brusque that Jennet stared, incensed by the lack of respect for a much-admired consultant surgeon who also happened to be Duncan Blair's boss!

Paul laughed, unperturbed. 'Valuable experience for you, man! Good training for when you step into my shoes—and that's what you're aiming for, isn't it? I like ambitious registrars,' he added smoothly. 'They do much of my work for me.'

'I don't object to the extra work, but I'm damned if I'll cover for you indefinitely.'

Jennet caught her breath, but Paul's smile never wavered. 'That sounds ominous,' he said lightly.

'It's meant to be. If you hadn't handed over when you did this morning I'd have felt compelled to ask you to stand down. If things don't improve very soon, I might feel equally compelled to take the matter to the Board.'

The grim threat hung in the air.

Shocked, Jennet looked from one man to the other as the newcomer threw down the curt challenge. Still smiling, Paul strolled to the door. 'I don't think there's any need to discuss our differences here and now, Duncan. Come and talk to me tomorrow,' he suggested smoothly.

The registrar turned away in disgust, balling his used towel with angry hands before hurling it into the bin. It wasn't the first time that he'd thrown down the gauntlet only to have it suavely brushed aside by a man who was as smooth and as slippery as an eel! But he was determined to speak out. He couldn't be the only one on Carter's firm to know about his drinking but it seemed that he was the only one prepared to bring it out into the open.

The consultant was regarded as some kind of

deity by his colleagues. Duncan had admired and respected his brilliant work for a very long time and it hurt to see a surgeon of such repute going steadily downhill. So, even at the risk of losing his job and endangering his own future, he meant to do what he could to save the situation.

Jennet glared at his broad back and hurried after Paul, catching up with him in the corridor. It was no place for a private conversation, with its bustle of nurses and porters and the rumble of trolley wheels, but she hurtled into anxious speech.

'Paul! I must talk to you! I've scarcely seen you since I got back from holiday and I'm worried about you. You don't look well and I'm sure you've lost weight. Can we meet this evening? Will you come to the flat for a meal and a chat?'

Overhearing the breathlessly urgent words as he emerged from the suite, Duncan couldn't fail to observe the intimacy between theatre sister and tall surgeon as she looked up at Carter with a plea in those beautiful eyes.

The consultant smiled back at her with an evasive warmth and Duncan felt a stab of suspicion combined with an unexpected distaste. Liking her blonde prettiness and trim figure and cool confidence, he might have taken steps to get on better terms with the attractive theatre sister, but he deplored her obvious association with a man twice her age.

About to hurry away, Paul glanced at his watch. 'I'm sorry, sweetheart. I can't make it this evening, I'm afraid. A medical dinner. I'll call you . . .'

He left her on the bland assurance and Jennet looked after him, troubled. He was avoiding the issue, she felt. He knew that she meant to challenge him about his drinking and he didn't want to discuss it. Duncan Blair had been harsh but he was probably right, she admitted with a very natural reluctance. If things didn't improve soon, the whole world would know that Paul was drinking too much and putting patients as well as his reputation at risk.

Turning, she saw the registrar surveying her with blatant disapproval. For no reason, the colour came up in her face and she saw his eyes harden. With a proud lift to her chin she stalked past him on her way to the changing-room.

He promptly fell into step at her side. 'Don't like me very much, do you, Sister?' he said mockingly. 'No one must say a word against the golden boy of the CU, is that it? Well, too bad if you won't face facts but he's a drunk and I'll shout it from the rooftops if it will protect his patients!'

'He's not a drunk,' Jennet refuted stonily, sick with hurt and dismay as the blunt words assailed her ears. 'He's had a bad time lately, that's all.'

'He lost his wife in a road accident. I know about that.' It was impatient.

'Everyone knows—but other people understand, make allowances . . .'

'Cover up for his mistakes, you mean! Well, I'm not prepared to do so when lives may be at stake, Sister,' he informed her bluntly. 'Maybe it isn't ethical to speak out against my boss but I'm not going to let him carve up patients like an incompetent because he's been hitting the bottle half the night and can't keep his hand from shaking!'

'How dare you say such things about him?' Jennet flared, unable to hold on to her temper for another moment. 'And to *me*!' Her hand flew to his cheek in furious assault.

Duncan caught her wrist in a bruising grip before the blow could connect. 'Oh, I realise that you're involved with the man,' he said censoriously. 'That's your business, of course. But it shouldn't blind you to the truth—and if you care about him that strongly then you should be doing your best to keep him sober!'

'Oh, you—you *idiot*!' she stormed, face flaming with anger and embarrassment and shock, near to hating the arrogant, self-righteous newcomer who had leapt to all the wrong conclusions. 'Of course I'm involved! Of course I care! He's my *father* . . .!'

CHAPTER TWO

'HE'S a pig! An arrogant, self-opinionated pig!'
Jennet fumed, still smarting from the clash of
furious faces and hissed words that had almost led
to blows regardless of their surroundings and
startled spectators, thankful that their paths hadn't
crossed again that day and that no one had been
tactless enough to refer to the incident in her
hearing.

Dr Verity Nesbit poured coffee into two cups and
pushed one across the table towards the flushed
theatre sister who had spilled the story of her
contretemps with the new registrar in an impulsive
outburst. 'I rather like him,' she said mildly. 'He's
very clever.'

'That doesn't excuse his appalling manners. Or
his nasty, suspicious mind!'

'You and Paul don't exactly behave like father
and daughter, on or off duty,' Verity pointed out
reasonably. 'Your obvious closeness can be
misleading to strangers, you must admit. As he
didn't realise the relationship, what else was he to
think?'

Jennet eyed her friend, puzzled by her readiness
to defend an obnoxious newcomer. Did Verity
fancy Duncan Blair? Surely not! She was much too
level-headed to be swayed by mere good looks and
masculine confidence!

'The man must be a fool if he's worked here for
three weeks and hasn't heard about Paul Carter's

daughter,' she said scornfully.

Verity shrugged. 'Of course he's heard. He just didn't know that he was sounding off about Paul to his daughter,' she reasoned. 'One theatre sister is much like another to a surgeon, and I don't suppose you were introduced to him by name.'

'We weren't introduced at all.'

'Well, then . . .'

Jennet admitted the fairness of the argument, but she was a long way from forgiving the man who had spoken so scathingly about her father—*and* cast aspersions on her own life-style! 'Well, *I* don't like him,' she said fiercely. 'And the less I see of Duncan Blair the better!'

'That may be difficult,' Verity suggested with a slight smile. 'Unless you're thinking of giving up theatre work?'

'Not to suit High and Mighty Blair!'

'What was it all about, anyway? I've only heard rumours . . .' Verity hadn't been present at the by-pass operation that morning, although she was attached to Paul Carter's team as a very junior doctor.

'Lots of those flying about, I suppose?' Jennet frowned.

'Well, of course. People are concerned. Paul's very well liked,' Verity said carefully.

She nodded. 'He isn't *well*, Verity. He hasn't really got over losing Frida and he's been working much too hard ever since. I mean to talk to him, see if I can persuade him to have a holiday. He desperately needs to get away for a while—and no doubt your clever Duncan Blair will be only too pleased to take over the reins for a month or two,' she added scathingly.

'It must be difficult for someone like Paul to admit that he isn't coping.'

Jennet sighed. 'He's lost and lonely and I don't know how to help. I wish I did.' She slumped wearily in her chair. It had been a long day. 'I'm his daughter. I'm his friend, too. But he just won't talk to me, Verity. He shuts me out . . .'

'Perhaps he doesn't want to upset you by talking about the accident.'

'Frida wasn't my mother.'

'I know that. But you were fond of her, surely?'

'Not really. I scarcely knew her before I came to London. I was thirteen when she and Paul married and she wasn't keen on the idea of a teenage daughter so I stayed in Wales. They quarrelled a lot, you know,' she added with sudden candour. 'Frida could be difficult at times, temperamental and demanding, like many actresses.'

'Wasn't she Swedish?'

'Yes. Very beautiful in a cold, rather superior kind of way.'

Verity hesitated. 'I don't think I ever heard what happened to your mother . . .' She was genuinely interested, not just curious.

'Oh, she died when I was a baby. My grandmother brought me up and I didn't see much of Paul until I began nursing. I expect that's why we really are friends rather than father and daughter.'

'You aren't much like him, either.'

'No. Apparently I resemble my mother.'

'They must have been very young when they married.'

'Paul was twenty, a medical student here at the Fitz, and my mother was a first-year nurse. I think she was only eighteen. They met and married in less than a month and horrified both families, apparently.' She smiled. 'It's hard to imagine Paul doing anything so madly impulsive, isn't it?'

Verity smiled, too. 'Don't you think he may be a romantic at heart?'

'Oh, yes! But he's so leisurely about most things. So cool, calm and collected.'

'On the surface,' Verity said meaningfully.

Jennet was pulled up short. She made a face. 'You're right, of course. He must be a whole mass of confused emotions behind that smiling façade. Or he wouldn't be drinking. I'm not talking about *social* drinking—everyone does that and I've never seen him the worse for it. But it's as though he *needs* to drink at times.'

'I dare say he does.'

'I don't mean that he's an alcoholic—or anywhere near it,' Jennet said hastily.

'Of course not.'

'I hate talking about him like this . . . it seems so disloyal. But you *knew*, anyway. Didn't you?' She sat up suddenly, intent on her friend's sympathetic face. 'I suppose everyone does,' she added wryly.

'Oh, I don't think so,' Verity soothed. 'It really isn't that noticeable—or that serious. Yet. But I do understand your concern, of course. He's such a fine man . . .' She broke off.

'He's a wonderful man! And I won't have that wretched Duncan Blair saying any different!' Jennet's anger bubbled up again.

Verity chuckled at the fierce blaze in the theatre sister's amber eyes. 'He must have been quite taken aback when you flew at him. That's where you *are* like Paul, you know. All serene on the surface and bubbling away underneath. Your nurses probably shake in their theatre shoes when you lose your temper!'

'It doesn't happen often. But that man . . .! I can't begin to tell you how I feel about him!'

'Poor Duncan. I'm sure he didn't realise that he was stirring up a hornet's nest.' Verity finished her coffee and pushed back her chair. 'Go home, have a long soak in a hot bath and put it all out of your mind,' she advised sensibly. 'I'm sure Paul doesn't want you to fight his battles for him and it seems a pity that you should be at loggerheads with his registrar over a misunderstanding.'

'It was no misunderstanding! He didn't even try to disguise the contempt he obviously feels for my father,' Jennet said hotly. 'And there wasn't the hint of an apology from the arrogant brute!'

'He always speaks very highly of Paul to me.'

Verity went to the door, realising that it was a waste of time to speak up for the new registrar while Jennet was in her present mood. For some reason, surgeon and theatre sister had taken a dislike to each other, and they would have to work it out for themselves. 'Oh, well, back to the grindstone. I'm beginning to wonder what it was about medicine that appealed to me,' she bemoaned lightly, stifling a yawn. It was her third consecutive week on duty with scarcely a break and she was clearly very tired.

'The thought of being surrounded by so many good-looking medical men, I expect.' Jennet forced a smile.

Verity laughed wryly. 'Who has time to notice? Or to date any of them?'

Jennet didn't follow her friend's well-meant advice. Going home to an empty flat just didn't appeal, she decided. She was still unsettled after her holiday and the events of the first day back at work meant that she would simmer and seethe about the impossible Duncan Blair for hours, as well as worry about Paul.

A film she had wanted to see for some time was showing at the cinema directly across the road from the hospital and she stubbornly sat through the whole of it, although the twin images of Paul and his new registrar kept coming between her vision and the screen.

It was dark when she made her way to the car park set aside for senior hospital staff, hunting for keys in her shoulder-bag. Unexpectedly, a tall figure materialised out of the shadows, directly in her path. She halted, every instinct shrieking a warning.

The light from a street lamp fell across Duncan Blair's powerful frame. 'Did I startle you? Sorry . . .'

He didn't sound sorry, and Jennet's mouth tightened. 'What do you want?' she demanded sharply.

He arched an eyebrow. 'What should I say to that? "Your money or your life?" It may surprise you, but I wasn't lying in wait to rob you of anything,' he drawled with unmistakable emphasis. 'I'm merely collecting my car.'

'At this hour?'

'I've been dealing with an emergency. Needless to say, I can't get hold of Paul and I doubt if he'd have been sober enough to operate if I'd managed to reach him.'

Jennet looked at the outspoken registrar with dislike, suspecting him of deliberate provocation. 'I advise you not to say such things about my father,

Mr Blair. I might be tempted to flatten you,' she said coldly.

A smile flittered across the lean, attractive face. 'Better men than you have tried and failed, Sister.'

'Looking at that nose, I doubt it!'

He laughed and stroked its slight irregularity with a rueful finger. 'Souvenir of my rugger days, Sister. I had enough sense to give up the game before it completely ruined my looks, however.'

'I'd have thought your *hands* were of more value!'

'They are, of course. But a badly battered surgeon doesn't impress the patients—or attract the nurses,' he said smoothly.

Impatient with his conceit, Jennet stalked towards her car. The registrar followed more slowly and she glowered at him over her shoulder before she realised that he was making his way to the car parked next to her own.

He strolled across to Jennet's Sierra as she slid behind the wheel. He rapped lightly on the closed car window with his knuckles. She ignored him, turning the key in the ignition to start the engine. He rapped again, peremptorily. Tempted to drive off and, preferably, *over* the arrogant surgeon, she wound down the window in obvious irritation.

'Well?'

The registrar held up a small leather wallet. 'Yours, I believe?'

Recognising the case that held her credit cards, Jennet instinctively reached for it in relief. 'Oh—yes! But where—how . . .'

Tantalisingly, he drew back his hand before she could claim her property. 'You pulled it out of your bag with your car keys. Very careless, Sister. Such cards are a gift to the unscrupulous, you know.

Lucky for you that I saw it fall.'

'I'm grateful.' Jennet spoke tersely, hand still outstretched.

'You don't sound grateful,' he reproached.

She gritted her teeth. 'It's late and I want to get home and I'm in no mood for games, Mr Blair.'

'Is it so hard for you to say thank you? Or did Paul fail to teach you the importance of good manners?' he mocked.

'*Thank you!*' Jennet ground out the words, a blaze of loathing for the detestable Duncan Blair in her amber eyes. 'Now, may I have my wallet?'

'For a kiss. That's fair exchange, isn't it?'

His face was in shadow. She couldn't see the laughter in his crinkled eyes or the twitch of his lips as he teased her, and she was deaf to the bantering note in that rich voice. She released the handbrake on a surge of fury. 'Keep it, damn you! I'll report the cards as lost . . .'

With a wry shake of his head, he tossed the wallet through the open window to land neatly in her lap. 'You've no sense of humour, Sister,' he reproached mockingly.

'Not where *you're* concerned!' Fuming, Jennet steered the Sierra towards the hospital gates as the surgeon shrugged and turned away to his own car. She was almost home before she began to calm down. He was impossible, infuriating, utterly hateful and much too sure of himself! It was obvious that he had no time for Paul—*or* his daughter. Well, she didn't like *him*, and for very valid reasons!

She lived on her own and liked it, although she had originally shared the apartment in Pilgrim House with a friend. The telephone was shrilling as she let herself in. She snatched up the receiver. 'Paul?' she asked hopefully, remembering his promise to call her.

'Hi, honey! I've been trying to get you all day at this number. Where in hell have you been?'

'Jeff? Jeff!' She said his name in breathless, incredulous astonishment.

'You haven't forgotten me, then?'

Jennet laughed shakily. 'How could I?' Her heart pounded with the shock of hearing from him. It was only days since they'd parted at the airport, but she had been sure that the flippant American had forgotten their holiday romance even before he reached the States. 'I've been at the hospital all day. I told you that I'm a nurse . . . Jeff, where are you ringing from, anyway? Washington?'

'Would you believe the London Hilton?'

'I'm not sure,' she said uncertainly, her heart missing a beat. It seemed unlikely, but one never knew with someone like Jeff. 'You're full of surprises . . .'

Well, this is another one for you! I'm over here on company business. Talked the old man into letting me handle it so we can get together again, Jennet. I said you hadn't seen the last of me and I meant it! Honey, I've missed you . . .' His voice dropped caressingly.

'It was fun, wasn't it?' Jennet said cautiously.

Running wild with a stranger was all very well for the Greek islands, but she didn't want it taken for granted that they would carry on where they had left off now that she was back on English soil—even if it was flattering that he'd apparently flown thousands of miles just to see her again. In spite of the intimacy of those days on the beach,

Jeff was still a stranger in many ways and she hadn't been completely swept off her feet by his good looks and his charm.

'I need to see my little English rose,' Jeff declared firmly. 'Shall I take a cab to your place? Or will you come join me here at the Hilton?'

'Jeff, I'm very tired,' she demurred. 'It's been a difficult day and I just want to fall into bed.'

'You're a mind-reader, honey! I'll be with you before your head touches the pillow!'

It was too light-hearted to be anything but banter. Nevertheless, a tiny tremor of alarm shook her at the words. 'You deserve a prize for persistence if nothing else,' she countered brightly.

'I didn't fly half-way across the world to have you go on saying no to me,' he warned, only half in jest. 'I sure don't know how you could resist me, all bronzed and beautiful in my Bermudas, but I just know that my new Eton suit will do the trick!'

Jennet laughed at the image conjured by the light words. 'Oh, Jeff—you *fool*! Eton suits are for schoolboys!'

'Is that a fact, ma'am?' he drawled.

'As if you didn't know! You're a dreadful tease!' she scolded.

'No, honey. You're the tease,' he returned deliberately.

Jennet felt uncomfortable at the reminder of the way she had disappointed him, time after time. She had been tempted to please him by summer kisses and warm, romantic nights beneath the stars but a natural caution had kept her from surrendering to a man she had only just met and wasn't at all sure that she was going to love for the rest of her life. Jeff might be convinced that she was his destiny, but holiday romances were more often the path to heartache than the key to lasting happiness, she had told herself sensibly.

'I don't mean to be,' she murmured, thankful that he couldn't see her glowing face. 'I just have to be sure . . .'

'*I'm* sure. Why aren't you?'

'Things happened so fast . . .'

'If it doesn't happen all in a moment then it may not happen at all,' he said sagely. 'It's called *falling* in love for a very good reason, Jennet.'

'People fall *out* of love all in a moment, too,' she reminded him.

'We aren't people, honey. We're the future Mr and Mrs Jefferson B. Lloyd! Hey, my old man can't wait to meet you! He's delighted that I'm going to take back a British wife.'

'Don't rush me, Jeff.' Jennet felt a stirring of panic and desperately tried to remember if she had ever agreed to marry him. As a result of drinking the very potent ouzo, perhaps! He'd proposed a dozen times during those few days. She knew she hadn't committed herself to anything, but he was talking as if they were practically engaged!

'You're one girl who just won't be rushed into anything, I guess.' It was wry.

'We need to know each other a lot better before we talk of marriage,' said Jennet firmly.

'Any way you want it, honey. Say! Listen to me! I'm already in training for the role of henpecked husband,' he laughed.

She drew a deep breath. 'I think you'll make a marvellous husband for some girl some day, Jeff. I'm just not yet sure that I'm meant to be that girl.'

'I'm over here for a month. That gives me plenty

of time to persuade you that I'm the only man for you.'

'A month! And I'm feeling guilty because I won't travel all the way across London to the Hilton at this hour! Jeff, I really am sorry but it's been a long day.'

'OK. I guess I'm a little jet-lagged myself,' he agreed placidly. 'We'll just have to paint the town all the colours of the rainbow tomorrow. I'll pick you up at that hospital where you're working—what's it called?'

'The Fitzroy. It's in North London.'

When arrangements had been made to meet the following day when she came off duty, Jennet put down the phone, her head in a whirl. She wanted to see Jeff again—of course she did! He had turned an ordinary holiday into an exciting adventure, and it was even more romantic that he had come all the way from Washington, USA, just to find her again. She ought to be dancing on air!

Making herself a hot drink and a sandwich, she wondered why she found it so hard to remember what Jeff looked like when it was less than a week since she had kissed him goodbye at the airport. He was dark and stocky and good-looking—but the only face she could apparently put to him belonged to a very different man.

Impatient, she brushed away the recurring image of Duncan Blair's harshly handsome features. It was vivid because of their more recent encounter, but the first had stamped him indelibly on her mind as a man to avoid.

Thank heavens for Jeff, uncomplicated, reliable, easy to know and like—and *love* . . .

* * *

Good morning, Sister.' Duncan Blair followed her into the lift in the morning and greeted her with cool courtesy.

Jennet nodded icily but didn't smile or speak as the doors slid shut and the lift began its slow ascent to the top floor and Theatres.

Ramrod-stiff, she stood as far from the surgeon as she could in that confined space, uncomfortably aware of him and avoiding those knowing grey eyes, irritated by a loose button that dangled from a thread on his suit sleeve. She was very conscious of his interested scrutiny and wished she were in uniform. Because she was meeting Jeff directly she went off duty, she had put on a suit that he had admired when she wore it on holiday, pretty and feminine and cool, with matching high-heeled shoes and evening purse tucked into the satchel-type bag that swung from her shoulder.

The registrar studied her shamelessly, his gaze sliding from the top of her bright hair to the tip of regulation black shoes, pausing to dwell with deliberate admiration on the thrust of taut breasts beneath the thin eau-de-Nil silk and the gentle rounding of hips in the fashionably short skirt, travelling the length of shapely legs, to come to rest finally on the flat-heeled brogues that ruined the effect of her chic appearance. The suggestion of amusement gleamed in his eyes.

Jennet stiffened.

'You look very elegant, Sister. Out to impress?' he suggested, smiling.

Her chin tilted. 'Not with you in mind!' she snapped unwisely.

He raised a sardonic eyebrow. 'I doubt if the patients will be in any condition to notice. But you'll certainly boost the morale of my fellow-surgeons!'

She brushed past him on her way from the lift, unwilling to analyse a rush of relief as she put distance between them but knowing that she felt oddly threatened by his maleness and his arrogant admiration.

'Even a dog's allowed one bite, Sister,' he murmured in her ear, catching up with her as she stalked towards the changing-room to exchange her finery for theatre greens.

Jennet recoiled from his sudden closeness, the warm rush of his breath against her neck, the waft of spicy and expensive aftershave and the unexpected tingle of her senses. 'I suppose that's as near as you'll get to an apology,' she said icily.

'I've no intention of apologising.' He looked down at her steadily. 'I meant everything I said about Paul, although I probably wouldn't have said it to you if I'd known you were his daughter—or not so bluntly, anyway. It must be obvious that I didn't mean to offend you. However, I'm willing to make amends. How about dinner?'

She stared at him in undisguised astonishment. He smiled at her as if he hadn't added insult to injury with the arrogance of that invitation. 'Are you serious? Do you really think I'd go out with *you*—for any reason? In any circumstances? You must be mad!' she declared hotly.

Duncan shrugged as the theatre sister stormed away. It *was* a kind of madness, he supposed. How else explain that he had spent much of the night thinking about the curve of her cheek, the sweetness of her mouth and those incredible eyes . . .?

CHAPTER THREE

JENNET walked into the scrub annexe some minutes later, still trembling, still incensed, still ready to do battle with the obnoxious Duncan Blair if he so much as looked at her in the wrong way.

He was arrogant and insensitive and utterly despicable. How dared he talk about taking her out after making that attack on Paul—not to mention the slur on her own morals and integrity! Did he really think she could overlook such insults? Never in a million years!

She tucked stray curls into her cap and glared at the man who was talking to Verity while she scrubbed. It annoyed her that her friend was beaming in response to the surgeon's smiling remarks. She was entitled to like him if she wished, but Jennet marvelled that Verity apparently *did*. She was fawning and fluttering over him like any first-year and Jennet turned away in sudden, angry impatience.

A whirlwind descended on the team of nurses responsible for getting the theatre ready that morning, criticising its cleanliness, sending some instruments back to the steriliser, demanding more swabs and more drapes and rounding on gossiping juniors who stared in open-mouthed astonishment at the usually sweet-natured theatre sister. They knew that she had a temper but it was carefully controlled and seldom vented on them, and each nurse searched her conscience for some clue as to

34

how she could have sinned. It was proof of Jennet's popularity that all the nurses were anxious to do well and win her approval.

'Hi . . .' Verity came up to her as she began to lay out instruments in readiness for the heart valve replacement that was the first procedure of the day. Theatre Three was allocated to the Cardiac Unit for three days a week and Jennet usually assisted as instrument nurse to one or other of the surgical teams. 'You went past me at the speed of light. Is anything wrong?'

'Everyone seems to be behind with their work this morning,' Jennet said crossly. 'If I don't keep these girls on their toes the whole place starts to fall apart!' She rounded on the first-year who had paused to help the new registrar to put on skin-tight surgical gloves with a great deal of shared amusement. 'Nurse Wilson, I need another general set—and that's the second time of telling! Please fetch it at once!'

With a startled glance at the snappish theatre sister, the disgruntled junior scurried away to get the extra instruments.

'One of those days?' Verity suggested with a sympathetic glow.

'No, I'm fine! Everything's fine!' Even Jennet realised that her tart tone belied the words and she had the grace to laugh at herself, 'Oh, dear! It doesn't sound like it, does it? I'm sorry, Verity. I didn't mean to bite your head off,' she said contritely.

'What is it?' Verity asked gently.

Jennet shrugged. Impossible to admit that Duncan Blair was at the root of her irritation. 'Oh, I'm just rushed . . . no, it isn't that, really!' She seized on a much more likely explanation for her unsettled frame of mind. 'Something's happened and I don't know whether to be pleased or not. I had such a surprise last night. Jeff's in London!'

'Your American?'

She wrinkled her nose. 'He *isn't*! Mine, I mean. He talks as if he'd like to be but I'm not sure . . .'

'You seemed sure enough a few days ago,' Verity reminded her, smiling. 'You were quite tearful at the thought that you'd probably never see him again.'

'Was I?' Jennet looked startled. 'I must have been carried away by all that sea and sand and sunshine—and he *is* nice, Verity. I *do* like him . . .' For all the emphasis, it was half-hearted. Surely, if Jeff had really captured her heart to any extent, she would remember him more clearly. As it was, his face was still a blur, she admitted wryly.

'But the magic dust has worn off,' Verity said with understanding.

'Blown away by the chill English breezes, I expect,' Jennet returned wryly. 'It's strange how romantic everything seems in a different climate.'

'And now it isn't romantic at all?'

'But it *is*—in a way.' Jennet was doing her best to be fair. 'Jeff seems to have wangled a business trip to London just to see me again—at least, that's what he says. To have come all this way does convince me that he *cares*—and he's so confident of marrying me before he goes back to the States that it almost frightens me,' she added on a rush of confidence.

Verity raised an eyebrow. 'He sounds like a very determined man. Or a juggernaut. But you aren't a weak person, Jennet. No one can hustle *you* into

doing anything that you don't want to do, I'm sure.'
She hadn't known the theatre sister for long, but
she felt that she knew her very well and, in common
with almost everyone at the Fitz, she liked her very
much.

'No. My grandmother says that I'm obstinate and
I expect that's true,' Jennet admitted.

'Strong-minded is so much more complimen-
tary,' Verity sympathised lightly.

Jennet smiled. 'Most men don't like women to
have a mind of their own, though, do they? Or to
do their own thing if it clashes with their plans?
Jeff's a dear but he's as chauvinist as most of them,
I suspect. He assumes that I'll give up nursing at
the drop of a hat to marry him and fly off to
America with him. He doesn't even ask how *I* feel
about it! I think he sees me in a frilly apron dishing
up delectable meals in a sparkling clean kitchen
for the lord and master on his return from a hard
day in the office. I don't think that's *me* at all!'

'It might be if you really loved him,' Verity said
shrewdly. 'I must say there are moments when I
think I'd rather be keeping house for some dishy
man than wearing myself out on the wards. Usually
in the darkest hour before the dawn of yet another
day on duty!'

Jennet finished checking the general set of
instruments supplied by the first-year. She smiled
at her friend and said lightly, 'Speaking of duty,
would you let Paul know that we're just about ready
for his patient? I haven't seen him around and he
ought to be scrubbing.'

'He isn't here yet. Duncan thinks he ought to
begin the procedure or the delay will build up and
affect the rest of the list. Duncan says these valve

replacements are fairly routine for someone with his amount of experience, anyway. He's letting me assist' she added, with satisfaction showing in the shine of her eyes. Newly qualified doctors spent months simply watching and learning and longing to assist the surgeons, and it was a feather in Verity's cap to be invited to act as second assistant.

'Heaven help the poor patient!' Jennet teased, but it hadn't improved her mood to have Duncan Blair's opinions quoted *ad nauseam* or to learn that she would be working in close physical contact with him that morning.

She was also anxious about Paul. It wasn't like him not to show up in good time to discuss the day's list with his team, and she wondered if he was ill. Or hungover.

Anxiety caused her to regard the registrar with an even more jaundiced eye as he walked into the operating-room, gowned and gloved and ready to take her father's place in the team. No doubt he would be delighted if Paul was forced to resign, she thought sourly. With his ambition and experience and colossal conceit, he probably saw himself as the natural successor to the consultancy.

If that ever came about, she would promptly hand in her own resignation, Jennet vowed fiercely. The man was insufferable as her father's registrar. She could never tolerate his arrogance and his attitudes if he had even more power and more say in the running of Theatre Three while it was her responsibility.

It wasn't easy to swallow her dislike of him enough to work at his side, handing instruments, swabbing where he indicated, following every move of his slightly unorthodox technique and ensuring that nurses were constantly on hand to run for fresh supplies. The surgeon was relaxed and confident, talking his way through the first part of the procedure, skilful hands busy in the cavity. Bristling, Jennet slapped scalpel or forceps or artery clamp into his hand almost before it was needed. Bridling, she followed each crisp, concise instruction to the letter. There was no way that she would give Duncan Blair the slightest cause to question or criticise her ability, she determined.

Suddenly the surgeon's hands were still. 'This is more complicated than we anticipated,' he said softly, a frown lurking in the grey eyes. The team listened intently as he went into lengthy detail and invited suggestions as to ways and means of solving the problem.

It was decided to break for coffee and more discussion while Jennet stayed to chat to Ben Drummond, who conscientiously monitored the patient until the surgeons returned. Duncan flexed strong, muscular hands in new gloves as he took up position beside the theatre sister. 'We've worked out a solution but it's likely to be a long job, I'm afraid. I hope your stamina is equal to your efficiency, Sister.'

Meeting a twinkle in the direct glance, Jennet was unaccountably flustered. He was laughing at her, but it was without malice and for a split second she warmed to him. She reminded herself hastily that she had no reason to like him and no intention of falling prey to his obviously practised charm. 'There's no need to worry about me, Mr Blair,' she assured him coolly. 'I'm used to working long hours in the theatre.' She reached blindly for the instrument she knew he needed and held it out, stiff with pride.

An eyebrow shot up in amused query. 'That doesn't look like a Spencer-Wells.'

Flushing and feeling foolish, she returned the Kelly haemostat to the tray and passed the artery forceps, cross with herself for confusing the two instruments in a moment of inattention.

'Take care, Sister. You run the risk of undermining your reputation as a first-class scrub nurse with such elementary mistakes,' Duncan drawled, unable to resist teasing the girl who was all starch and unbending resentment.

Jennet stiffened as Tim Gowan stifled a snort of laughter and nurses exchanged amused glances; even Ben looked up from the patient with the gleam of a smile in his eyes. She was furious with the registrar for making fun of her. She made no answer, but she looked her loathing.

He might think her sullen, but she couldn't bear to be teased on something so sensitive as her professionalism by a newcomer whom she instinctively disliked.

Duncan's light words concealed a growing impatience with the humourless girl whose attitude threatened to create an impossible situation. He might eventually find it intolerable to work with her—and that would be a pity because she *was* a first-class scrub nurse, deft and quick and reliable. A good working relationship was essential when so many hours were spent together in the operating theatre. Tension between surgeon and theatre sister didn't help anyone, least of all the patient!

Paul strolled into the theatre half-way through the operation. 'Damn traffic gets worse,' he announced with a nonchalance that didn't deceive his registrar or his daughter. 'Glad you didn't wait for me . . . how's it going?' He peered over the surgeon's broad shoulder.

Duncan didn't look up, hands busy in the cavity. 'We hit a snag.' Briefly, he explained the method he was using to overcome it.

Paul nodded. 'I thought we might run into that particular problem in that area,' he said sagely, but he didn't add that a doubt as to his ability to cope with it, together with the need to recover from the drinking jag of the previous night, had delayed his arrival.

Watching his registrar's sure, skilled hands, he felt a twinge of envy. He knew that his own days as a surgeon were numbered unless he mastered the need for the alcohol that numbed pain and guilt, restored his spirits if only temporarily, and renewed a diminished confidence in his ability.

'Want to take over at this point?' Duncan paused while Jennet wiped a trickle of sweat from his face. He was reluctant to hand over to someone who didn't look fit to wield a scalpel but it *was* Carter's patient, after all.

'No, no. Carry on,' Paul urged blandly. 'You seem to be doing all the right things, and I'm sure Mr Snow is in good hands.'

Duncan saw a glimmer of concern in beautiful amber eyes as the theatre sister shot a glance at her father. He felt a wave of sympathy for her situation. She was bound to be loyal and protective, but as a trained nurse she must admit that Carter's drinking bouts made him a danger to his patients and a liability in the operating theatre. However, the proud and pretty Sister Carter wasn't likely to admit it to *him*!

'Everything all right at your end, Ben?' he automatically checked before proceeding.

The anaesthetist looked up briefly from his preoccupation with monitoring the flow of by-passed blood. 'He's in pretty good shape at the moment.'

Paul turned to the youngest member of the team who was keeping a firm grip on a retractor, too intent on her task to acknowledge him with more than a fluttering glance. 'Assisting, Verity? That's a new experience for you, isn't it?' he said indulgently.

'She's earned it,' Duncan said shortly. 'She's been worked into the ground lately with little reward.'

'Oh, I'm all in favour of encouraging the young,' Paul approved silkily. 'Gives them a chance to show what they can do.'

'Verity's doing very well, in fact. A very useful pair of hands.' The warm tribute was accompanied by the gleam of a smile in grey eyes.

Verity glowed with gratitude for the friendly acceptance that compensated in part for the very hurtful patronage of the consultant's attitude.

That smiling glance, and Verity's swift sparkle of response to it, gave Jennet a shock of surprise. She hadn't realised until that moment that her friend's warm defence of the new registrar sprang from something more than mere liking. It seemed to be a mutual attraction, too, for no one could mistake the admiration behind the praise. Perhaps they had got to know each other more intimately than Verity was admitting in the few weeks since Duncan Blair had taken up his appointment to the Cardiac Unit.

Verity claimed to be interested in medicine rather than men and the long, unsocial hours of her job certainly left her little time or energy for dating. Tired and dispirited by the demands of a junior doctor's life in a busy general hospital, perhaps she had been ripe to fall into Duncan Blair's undoubtedly unscrupulous hands. But Jennet was puzzled by her friend's penchant for the man. He was undeniably a charmer, but she suspected that the coldness of those steel-grey eyes at times reflected an uncaring heart in spite of an obviously sensual nature. He was the type who took all and gave nothing, she decided sweepingly, convinced that he was the last man she would want in *her* life and hoping that Verity hadn't fallen too heavily for his dangerous brand of charm.

Jennet stole a glance at her father from time to time. His mask hid most of his handsome face and his sombre eyes gave no clue to his thoughts or feelings, but she sensed his disquiet. It was unlike him to delegate the responsibility for a patient to a colleague, however clever. Either he wasn't feeling well enough to operate—or he didn't trust himself to do it efficiently. Another hangover?

She saw a glint of approval in his dark eyes as she assisted with the final suturing. He liked to see her working in harmony with his registrar, she realised. Did he feel that they made a good team? They had worked well together, needing few words, hands and minds in unison and sharing a caring concern for the patient on the table. Her admiration for the skilful technique of a fine surgeon had temporarily overcome her feelings about the man, she admitted.

Intent as he was on improving the quality of life for the patient, Duncan Blair's natural arrogance had been subdued and Jennet had forgotten her dislike of him as hand touched hand in the passing of scalpel or forceps or diathermy needle. She had glowed when he approved an intuitive perception of his requirements with the quick glance or nod that was all that he allowed to interrupt his concentration. So she was unprepared for the cool dismissal in his manner as she snipped the last suture and he tossed the needle-holder into a bowl.

'That's it! He'll do,' he said confidently. 'Thank you, Sister—do the dressing, would you?' He turned from the table, pulling down his mask, smiling at the young doctor who eased her stiff weariness with a stretch and a sigh. 'Well done, Verity! We'll make a surgeon of you in no time.' He put an arm about her shoulders in a brief, affectionate hug. 'As a token of my admiration, I'll buy you a drink when we've finished the list.'

'I'll hold you to that!' Verity laughed, but her glance slid towards the consultant whose dark eyes had narrowed at the exchange of warm words, warm glances.

Paul smiled indulgently and strolled towards the scrub annexe. Jennet's hands were busy with dressing the wound but her eyes were on the couple who followed her father from the operating-room. She felt a fierce stab of irritation with Verity's foolish, fawning and totally feminine response to Duncan Blair's arrogant approval. As if that massive ego needed boosting, she thought crossly.

Mr Snow was wheeled away to Intensive Care, surrounded by drips and an array of monitors. Jennet began the preparations for the next procedure, feeling aggrieved. She had worked with a number of celebrated surgeons during her years at The Fitz and they had all courteously praised her ability and thanked her for her assistance. That cool word of thanks from a mere registrar seemed poor return for all her hard work and efforts to please that morning!

She didn't want or expect Duncan Blair to buy *her* a drink at the end of the day, as he had promised Verity with a smile that must have quickened her pulses, but a little appreciation would have been welcome, she told herself on a stir of resentment.

Bustling in and out of the annexe with a chip on her shoulder that the registrar probably didn't notice, she overheard Tim Gowan's suggestion that the last and least urgent case on the list should be postponed.

'We're running about two hours behind schedule,' he ventured.

'It isn't my way of doing things,' Duncan said brusquely. 'I'd need a really good reason for disappointing a patient at such short notice. In my book, we work to the end of the list. Or drop!'

'I guess so . . .' But Tim didn't look too happy.

'Too bad if it interferes with your social life.' It was unsympathetic. 'You chose surgery and you can't walk out in the middle of a procedure just because the clock says you ought to be off duty. It's different for theatre sisters, of course,' he added with a glancing smile for the girl who was busy in a corner. 'You won't need to keep *your* date waiting, Sister. Someone will take over from you in good time, no doubt.'

Paul turned, breaking off his conversation with Verity on the other side of the room. '*Do* you have a date, Jennet?' He sounded slightly disgruntled. 'I wish I'd known. I've booked a table at Lester's.'

It was her favourite restaurant. She wanted time with Paul, too, to talk, to get closer to him if she could, and she would have ensured that he didn't drink too much in her company, she thought, noticing the sallow hue of his complexion and the slightly bloodshot eyes. But she had promised Jeff . . . 'I wish I'd known,' she echoed drily. 'But I've arranged to meet someone tonight.'

'Anyone I know?' Paul asked promptly.

'No. Someone I met on holiday, actually. He's an American,' she said reluctantly, aware that Duncan Blair was listening with undisguised interest.

'Bring him along,' Paul said expansively.

Jennet hesitated. She wanted them to meet, and dinner with her distinguished father would certainly ease any awkwardness she might feel about being with a near-stranger without the beauty and charm of the Greek islands that had turned a holiday flirtation into a romance. A few days had made a surprising difference to her feelings, she realised. She had been ready, almost eager, to love Jeff and to shape her life about him when he kissed her, murmuring hopes and dreams for the future, as they lay on the beach or stood under the stars within sight and sound of the shimmering sea. Now, back among friends and in familiar surrounds, doing the job she loved, she was far from sure that it was what she really wanted, after all.

But perhaps her heart would quicken with the confidence of loving as soon as she saw Jeff again . . .

'We'll leave it for the moment, if you don't mind,' she said lightly. 'I'm sure Jeff has already made plans for the evening.' With a glow of her golden smile, she went on with her work, knowing that a blush had stained her cheeks, making Jeff seem more important to her than he actually was as yet.

The list was finished almost on schedule in spite of Tim Gowan's fears, and the surgical team left to change. Jennet stayed to supervise the cleaning of the theatre and the sterilising of instruments, going off duty some time later to change before meeting Jeff in Main Hall. Verity was hanging about in the corridor. As Duncan Blair came out of the surgeons' changing-room, Jennet realised that her friend was waiting for the registrar. No doubt they were going for that drink, she thought with a surge of annoyance at Verity for pandering to the man's insufferable conceit.

There was an animal grace about his long, lithe stride and a hint of leonine power in those broad shoulders. A slant of sunlight fell across his handsome head with its mane of chestnut hair and strong, rugged features. He was attractive, Jennet grudgingly conceded, observing the warmth of his swift smile for the young doctor. Even from a distance, she felt all the impact of its charm. She didn't believe that hearts *could* turn over, but hers certainly behaved very oddly for a moment.

Cross with herself for a stab of envy as the surgeon put an arm about Verity and took her with him out of the Unit, she rushed into the changing-room to strip off her greens and step under a shower to sluice away not only all trace of the long day from hair and skin but also the absurd hankering for a man she didn't even *like*! Duncan Blair had absolutely no attraction for her except the physical—and she sternly crushed the sudden, startling sweep of desire that threatened to undermine her determination to have nothing to do with the new registrar above and beyond the demands of her job . . .

CHAPTER FOUR

JENNET'S heart raced with a mix of excitement and trepidation as she scanned the vast, high-ceilinged Main Hall and wondered, a trifle foolishly, if she would know Jeff among the crowd of patients and relatives and staff in mufti.

Hurrying the last few yards, breathless with anticipation, she swung at a touch on her shoulder, glowing with a delight that promptly faded at sight of the man who had moved so swiftly to intercept her.

'Oh, not *now*!' she snapped with an instinctive recoil from the impressive height, striking good looks and powerful personality of the new registrar. 'I'm on my way to meet someone . . .'

'And you won't keep him waiting even for a moment? Lucky man,' Duncan drawled, his appreciative gaze consuming the girl in the soft-hued suit that set off her fair loveliness so well. He was enchanted by her lovely face and figure and the golden smile that she seemed to bestow on everyone but himself and he found himself seriously envying the man she was hurrying to meet. What had begun as a mild stir of interest was rapidly becoming a wild flame of desire for a girl who kept him at bay with the militant sparkle in her amber eyes.

'It depends what you want.' Her tone was impatient and her glance anxiously sought Jeff but she seemed rooted to the spot by the registrar's compelling presence. Why couldn't she just walk away from him? And what was he doing here, waylaying *her*, when she had last seen him ushering Verity from Theatres with a brilliant smile and that casually possessive arm about her friend's shoulders?

It wasn't the moment to tell her that he wanted to whisk her out of this crowded, aseptic building and take her to some place where they could talk and laugh and make love and get to know each other as well as destiny surely intended. Just now, her head was full of another man. Duncan was determined to oust that unknown rival if it took every trick in the book.

'Just a word, Sister.' His smile held all the warmth that had drawn women to him in the past. 'Some good advice. It isn't wise to get too involved with a stranger met by chance in a foreign country. There are some unsavoury characters about these days.'

He was genuinely concerned, although her attitude didn't encourage him to care what happened to her. A virginal quality gave a special touch to her blonde beauty and it was part of her appeal to him and other men. A less scrupulous man might not have hesitated to take advantage of that rare innocence. Duncan sensed a slumbering passion beneath the cool exterior that had probably kept many men at a distance. Once awakened, it might sweep her into the wrong arms.

Jennet caught her breath at the effrontery of the words. What right did he have to offer advice, good or bad? Wasn't he even more of a stranger than Jeff—and even more of a danger, if her instincts could be trusted!

'I don't believe I'm hearing this!' she said angrily.

'You know nothing about the man I'm meeting!'

'Do you know much more?' Duncan countered shrewdly. 'Holiday romances may be exciting, but they seldom last and they can lead to a lot of trouble.'

'Voice of experience?' she asked acidly.

He brushed aside the jibe with a hint of impatience. 'Casual affairs of that nature have never appealed to me. I'm not promiscuous.'

Jennet gasped. 'And you think I *am*!'

The smile that tugged at his sensual mouth betrayed none of his regret at an unfortunate choice of words. 'No. Just impulsive, perhaps—and that puts you at risk, in my opinion,' he said smoothly.

'I don't give a damn for your opinions!' She was incensed by the arrogant assumption that she needed to be protected from her own emotions.

Duncan shrugged in response to the expected show of spirit. 'OK. But what *do* you know about him? He may be a drug-dealer or a gun-runner . . .'

'Or a white-slaver?' she jeered, amber eyes flashing contempt for the absurdity of all such suggestions. 'You're living in the past. This is *now*—and I'm quite capable of taking care of myself in any situation. I certainly don't need your unwanted advice!'

As she turned away, the surgeon checked her with a peremptory hand on her arm. 'Wanted or not, here's some advice you shouldn't ignore,' he said sternly. 'Let him know you have friends who care what happens to you. In fact, it might be as well if he sees us together and then you can introduce me . . .'

Jennet shook off the hand that seemed to burn

her flesh through the filmy sleeve. 'As a *friend*?' She smiled with cool contempt. 'You must be joking, Mr Blair. I can do without friends like you!' She stalked away, head high, trembling with a reaction that could only be anger. Seeing Jeff, so instantly familiar that she marvelled at her doubts, she rushed to meet him with an eagerness that cocked a snook at the watching surgeon.

Duncan Blair could issue any number of dire warnings but there was no reason why *her* holiday romance shouldn't turn into a lasting love-affair, she thought defiantly. She looked at Jeff's solid, sturdy frame and clean-cut good looks and honest blue eyes and decided that she could trust her own judgement. After all, she hadn't reached the ripe old age of twenty-four without meeting a few bad guys. Jeff wasn't one of them, she felt, sure that he meant every word of the heartwarming things he said to her.

Perhaps it *had* happened very quickly, the bud of liking blossoming in the Greek sunshine to a full-blown rose of romance, and perhaps they *didn't* know too much about each other as yet. But wasn't it possible that Jeff loved her just as much as he said—and just as possible that the warmth of her feeling for him could grow into real and lasting love?

'Who was that guy?' Jeff asked suspiciously, steering her towards the street.

'Nobody! Just one of the surgeons . . .' Jennet dismissed Duncan Blair and his cautions with the airy words, hugging Jeff's arm as they left the building. 'It's so good to see you,' she said with all the impulsiveness that the registrar had unerringly detected in her nature.

She was impressed with Jeff's appearance, the well-cut suit and discreet shirt and tie, the neat haircut and careful grooming of the man she had only seen in jeans or shorts with colourful T-shirt or bare-chested, body bronzed by sun and sea. Now, he looked the successful businessman he claimed to be instead of an itinerant beachcomber, she thought, with an admiring rush of relief that swept away doubts implanted by another man's words.

'It's great to be with you, too, honey. It would have been worth swimming right across the Atlantic Ocean to see you again,' Jeff declared with extravagant but slightly absent flattery as he flagged a passing taxi.

'We can use my car . . .' Jennet demurred.

He shook his head. 'I've had experience of trying to park in this city and it isn't worth the hassle. It's easier to use cabs.' He slid across the cool leather seat towards her and took her into his arms. 'Besides, it leaves a man's hands free to touch his girl,' he added softly.

His lips were warm and gently seeking and Jennet waited for the magic, the lift of her heart and the quickening of her pulses, the melting of her flesh. Perhaps it was the stuffy, smoky interior of the taxi, the distraction of traffic noise and the lingering weariness of the long day in Theatres, but she found herself forcing the response that he obviously expected.

As his caressing hand slid from her throat to the swell of her breast beneath the sliding silk, stroking and kneading, his kiss deepened and demanded. Tensing, she shrank from the too-intimate touch and covered his hand with her own, stilling the seductive caress that didn't stir her.

'Not now, Jeff,' she whispered with a warning glance at the taxi-driver, who was conscientiously keeping his eyes from the mirror that reflected his passengers. With the warm tone she did her best to soften the rebuff.

'You weren't such a prude on the beach,' he grumbled, lips on her hair, nibbling the lobe of her ear, nuzzling the sweet hollows of her neck.

Jennet sighed as he gripped her shoulder with a strong hand and drew her closer, continuing to make light love to her with lips and eyes and murmured endearments as if she hadn't protested. There was more than a grain of truth in his reproach. Somehow, it had seemed so natural that he should kiss and fondle her bare breasts as they lay in the sun or swam together in the warm sea. Somehow, it hadn't seemed dangerous to kindle desire in this easygoing, kindly man. Somehow, she had felt herself in control, because it was such light-hearted lovemaking and he had obeyed as soon as she called halt.

But now she felt that they had stepped beyond the line where she could continue to keep him at bay. That worried Jennet. Perhaps she *was* a prude. She knew it was old-fashioned to insist on loving a man before going to bed with him, but she clung to the conviction that sex for her would only be right and good when it happened with a man she wanted to love for the rest of her life. She still wasn't sure that Jeff was that man.

Wriggling out of his embrace, she rubbed her shoulder with a rueful laugh. 'I'll be black and blue tomorrow! You don't seem to know your own strength!'

Jeff cradled her face in both hands and looked intently into guarded amber eyes. '*You* don't seem to know how strongly I feel about you,' he returned quietly. 'I'm madly in love with you, Jennet—and I won't go back to the States without you, come hell or high water!'

The flutter of her heart ought to have been delight. But Jennet took fright at the force of resolution behind the words. How would Jeff take it if she decided that she couldn't love him and didn't want to marry him? Would he be angry, accusing her of leading him on only to let him down? Would he be difficult, insisting, pestering, refusing to fade gracefully from her life—and could she handle such a situation? She found so much comfort in the thought that he was only in London for a month that it seemed her liking for the American wasn't about to turn into love.

But her emotions had been so upset by his unexpected arrival that it would take some time for them to settle—and in a few weeks she might be very happy to settle for the man she had met on holiday. Every woman dreamt of being loved by a man who would dare all for her sake, and he was a very romantic knight, with his impetuous dash half-way across the world to find her again and his eagerness to sweep her into his arms and take her back to America with him. He was kind and generous and good-natured and the only son of a wealthy industrialist—what more could any girl want?

He was good company, too. After tea at Fortnum's, they strolled in Green Park before taking a taxi to the Embankment to look at the Thames as it flowed beneath London's famous bridges. They went on to see the lions in Trafalgar Square and visited the National Gallery to look at portraits of people that Jeff claimed almost convincingly as ancestors. Later, as it grew dark, they walked hand in hand around Piccadilly and Leicester Square and finally, tired but elated, smiled at each other across a table in a small but excellent Greek restaurant.

She was surprised to realise that Jeff knew London much better than she did, although she had explored much of the city in the six years that she had worked at the Fitz. She knew all the famous landmarks, of course . . . St Paul's and the Tower of London, Buckingham Palace, the Houses of Parliament. She had window-shopped in the splendid malls of Piccadilly and Bond Street and Knightsbridge. She had been to many of the theatres and cinemas as well as some of the better restaurants and clubs with her friends. But Jeff's intimate knowledge of the side streets, the dark quarters of Soho, the small clubs and cafés tucked away in quiet corners, betrayed that he was no stranger to the secret life behind London's bright lights.

He was obviously well known to the proprietor of the restaurant where they drank ouzo and enjoyed a selection of Greek dishes. Jennet had already discovered that he was fluent in a number of languages. He was a surprising man in some ways and that emphasised how little she knew about him, Jennet told herself sensibly. As she had said, she needed to know a lot more about Jefferson B. Lloyd before she could seriously consider him as a husband. Yet she knew that if she had fallen headlong into love with him on that beautiful island in the sun, she would be taking him very much on trust . . .

Jeff sat slightly apart from her in the taxi that sped them through quiet suburban streets to her apartment shortly after midnight, saying little, and she supposed that he was tired, like herself. She wondered what would happen when they were finally alone and she had no good excuse for saying no to him. It was unlikely that he would be content with kisses now, she thought wryly, wishing that she was sure enough of her feelings and the future to offer more.

Catching her doubtful glance, Jeff smiled and pursed his lips in a kiss that he made no move to deliver. Jennet wondered if she was freezing the poor man with the cool reserve that sprang from a sudden shy uncertainty. She recalled the carefree intimacy of those days on the beach when he had kissed and caressed her like a lover and she had revelled in the romance of a chance encounter and its outcome. She had thought him the man of her dreams. Now, he seemed like a stranger.

He handed her down from the taxi outside Pilgrim House and turned to speak to the driver. Jennet waited, suddenly dry-mouthed with apprehension.

Jeff took her arm and turned her towards the building. 'I told the cabby to wait.'

'Then you aren't staying . . .?' She did her best to keep the relief from her tone.

'If I thought that that was an invitation I'd take you up on it,' he grinned. 'But I know you better, honey. You're an old-fashioned girl, and I'm not going to rush you and risk losing you.'

Impulsively, Jennet moved close and put her

arms about him. He was so nice, so understanding and thoughtful. 'You're welcome to a nightcap,' she assured him on a twinge of guilt.

'I'm booked to meet a guy for a drink, back at the hotel,' he said unexpectedly. 'We met on the plane coming over. He's in the same line of business and he's promised to cut me in on a good deal.' He brushed her cheek with his lips and smiled into her eyes. 'So go get your beauty sleep, sweetheart . . .'

Jennet didn't believe he was meeting anyone at such a late hour. He was just saving face and making things easy for her, she decided gratefully.

She was really very fond of him, she thought warmly, watching the tail-light of the taxi disappear into the night. But, deep down, she knew that he wasn't destined to be the love of her life . . .

Choosing items for her lunch in the self-service hospital cafeteria, she saw Verity waving to her from a table by the window. They were both busy and it was the first time that their paths had crossed that day, so Jennet carried her tray across the room to join her friend. 'How did you find time to eat?' she teased.

'I think someone felt sorry for me,' the young doctor quipped. 'I expect I look like a zombie.'

'You look remarkably fresh, in fact.' There were smudges of weariness beneath Verity's eyes but there was a hint of colour in her usually pale face and she seemed to radiate a renewed zest for life after the long-awaited night off duty. 'Oh, to be twenty-two again,' Jennet sighed in mock envy, eyes twinkling.

Verity smiled. 'I feel forty! How was your evening?' she asked, forestalling a similar enquiry.

'Marvellous! We went to a Greek restaurant in Soho for dinner. The place and the people brought back all the holiday memories and the food was out of this world!' With an expressive wrinkle of her nose, Jennet turned over the tired lettuce leaf and the watery tomato that was the cafeteria's excuse for a salad.

'I gather that Jeff's just as nice as you found him on holiday?'

'Oh, nicer!' Jennet had gone to sleep thinking about the evening she had spent with Jeff and had woken that morning wondering why she had kept him out of her arms when he was just the kind of man she had always dreamt of loving and marrying. She *was* a prude—or frigid, which was worse!

'So it's to be wedding bells in the near future?' Verity searched her friend's face for some clue as to how the evening had ended. Jennet looked exactly the same as always but would she look any different if she had spent the night in a man's arms? Did *she*?

'Oh, I don't think so,' Jennet demurred, laughing. 'Not too soon, anyway!'

Her heightened colour and the sparkle in amber eyes hinted otherwise to the man who sat nearby, apparently unnoticed by either girl but able to hear every word that passed between them.

A cooling cup of coffee was in front of Duncan, together with the *Lancet* that had lost his attention when he saw the slender girl in the short green theatre frock making her way across the cafeteria with a sunny smile for her friend. He had been startled by an unexpected catch at his heart and a stir of longing.

He seldom used the hospital cafeteria but he had dropped in for coffee and a sandwich before beginning the afternoon rounds, his time too limited for a proper lunch. Now, he made himself as unobtrusive as he could so that the theatre sister wouldn't become aware of him and begin to guard her conversation—no easy feat for a man of his height and build!

With the medical journal raised to conceal his interest, Duncan unashamedly eavesdropped, looking over the top of the *Lancet* at the lovely, animated face and the bright curls that gleamed in the sunshine streaming through the wall of plate-glass window that bordered the cafeteria. He was anxious to know more about Jennet Carter's feeling for the man she had met on holiday. Perhaps it was foolish and unnecessary but he was concerned about where that affair was leading an obviously impulsive girl. It could be happiness for her at the end of the road. It could just as easily be heartbreak—and it might to be to his advantage to be around to pick up the pieces.

Verity's radiopager bleeped across Jennet's enthusiastic description of the American's good looks and many attractive qualities. 'Duty calls . . .' Relieved from the beginning of boredom with a man she had yet to meet, she rose to her feet with a wry grimace and hurried across to a wall-mounted telephone to take the message that probably recalled her to the Cardiac Unit.

Jennet exchanged smiles with her as Verity hurried from the cafeteria with an apologetic wave, and then she turned back to her unappetising lunch. For the first time, her glance fell on the registrar.

Perhaps he construed that glance and the remnant of her smile as an invitation. Or perhaps he was just in the habit of pushing himself forward, wanted or not, she thought crossly, as he promptly closed the medical journal he was reading and came to join her, sliding his tall frame into Verity's vacated seat.

Jennet looked at him without welcome.

'No appetite, Sister?' He indicated her virtually untouched meal.

'Not any more,' she said pointedly, laying down her fork.

Duncan smiled. 'Why eat here if you don't like the food?'

Jennet shrugged. 'I'm an optimist. I always think it may have improved since last time.'

'The pub is more reliable.'

'More crowded, too.'

He nodded. 'There's a shortage of eating-places in the area, unfortunately. But we could always go further afield for a meal.' He smiled at her. 'I hoped to run into you.'

'I hoped *not* to run into you,' Jennet riposted sweetly, ignoring the odd flip of her heart at that lightly worded invitation. She avoided the sudden smoulder in the surgeon's grey eyes, strangely flustered and slightly breathless and much too aware of him. He was so *physical*, she thought with a surge of resentment, disturbed by the dark sexuality of the man.

Duncan Blair found her attractive, she realised in a shock of mingled dismay and excitement. He would sweep her into bed if she gave him half a chance—and she ought to be outraged by the desire she sensed in his powerful frame. Instead, an answering quiver of longing stirred, deep down, insistent.

She looked at his hands, spread on the table, strong and sensitive and well-shaped, surgeon's hands that dealt so skilfully with scalpel and suture needle and were probably just as skilful at stirring and exciting a woman to undreamed-of heights of pleasure. His touch might easily tempt her to forget everything but the delight he promised with the way he looked and smiled and spoke, Jennet admitted to herself on another shocking dart of desire.

Against her will, she was drawn to look up into penetrating grey eyes that seemed to see into the very heart of her and recognise the response to his magnetism that she really couldn't help. He was the most attractive man she had ever known, Jennet thought, catching her breath. The rich chestnut hair tempted fingers to thrust through its thick waves and curls, and she longed for his eyes to warm with liking and tenderness as well as that alarming desire. The breadth of his shoulders promised strength and reliability, and the powerful body with its hint of leashed passion ensured a breathtaking ecstasy for any woman who welcomed his ardent lovemaking.

For the first time, Jennet understood that it wasn't necessary to love a man to ache for his embrace, to yearn for his kiss or to melt and mould her body in willing response to the urgent heat of his passion.

It was all a matter of chemistry—and if Jeff had inspired only a little of the wild flurry of wanting that swept her as she met Duncan Blair's challenging gaze, she would have been in bed with him days before, she thought inconsequentially . . .

CHAPTER FIVE

'I KNOW how you feel about me, Sister.'

The direct words sent such a bolt of alarm through Jennet that she dropped the teaspoon she had been rotating in restless fingers. It clattered noisily on the Formica-topped table between them and the surgeon shot out a hand to silence it.

'And I'm about to make matters worse,' he swept on with no trace of regret.

She visibly relaxed on a rush of relief that her eyes hadn't betrayed her thoughts. 'I doubt if you could,' she returned sweetly. 'You're right at the bottom of my Christmas card list, as it is.'

Duncan didn't smile. 'You won't like what I have to say. I'm going to say it, anyway.'

Jennet shrugged. 'Feel free . . .' Her glanced roamed the cafeteria with an airy indifference to the criticism or complaint she expected him to voice.

'I suppose you're aware of your father's association with Verity Nesbit? Isn't it time that you did something about it?'

She had expected anything but *that*, and her eyes flew to his face in astonishment. He was serious, very determined, and now there was no trace of the elemental passions that had troubled her only moments before. 'Paul and Verity . . .?' she echoed, bewildered.

'People are talking,' he warned curtly. 'The pair of them are damnably indiscreet at times. Paul seems to have some kind of death-wish where his work and his reputation are concerned.'

'I don't know what you're talking about . . .' But, even as she protested, things were falling into place. Verity's eagerness to bring Paul's name into almost every conversation, her quiet but persistent interest in everything about him, her frequently voiced admiration and sympathy and concern, the way her face lit up when he walked into a room. Jennet marvelled that she had been blind and deaf for so long to an obvious infatuation.

But Duncan Blair was hinting at more than a young girl's infatuation for an older man, she realised with shock.

Duncan watched the play of reaction across her lovely, expressive face. 'I think you do,' he said quietly. 'I think you encourage her interest, and he certainly doesn't hesitate to exploit it.'

Amber eyes sparked indignation. 'Are you saying that Verity's having an affair with *my father?*' Jennet was startled and dismayed but, more than anything else, she was angered by the suggestion that *she* had fostered such an affair. Why would she, for heaven's sake? What could Paul and Verity possibly give each other when twenty years and a wealth of experience separated them?

Duncan shrugged.

The lift of those broad shoulders was so expressive that Jennet looked at him coldly. 'It's an absurd accusation. But even if there were any truth in it, I don't see that it's any of *your* business.' Why *was* he so concerned? she wondered crossly. Was he jealous? Did he have plans of his own for Verity?

She was good-looking and bright and very good at her job—the ideal wife for an ambitious surgeon, perhaps? He obviously liked Verity, and Jennet was sure that his interest in her friend had nothing in common with his blatantly sexual attitude to herself. No doubt he saw Verity as the kind that a man might marry, while *she* was the kind that a sensual man took to bed and promptly forgot, she thought bitterly.

'It ought to be *your* business,' Duncan said bluntly. 'I don't know if you've any influence with either of them, but there must be something you can do to prevent your friend from making a fool of herself and your father from wrecking the career of a promising young doctor.'

'You're assuming a great deal, aren't you?' Jennet challenged. 'I know Verity admires my father, but I'm sure that there's no more to it than that. And Paul wouldn't make love to a girl half his age. You're just leaping to conclusions. *Again!*'

'I'm not wrong this time,' he said flatly.

'You're wrong about me, for a start!' A flooding resentment tinged the words, surprising the surgeon with their vehemence. Seeing the arch of a startled brow, Jennet hastened to redeem the proud reproach. 'What makes you think that I'd encourage such an affair, anyway?'

'I think you feel that Verity will be good for him, give him a new interest, perhaps keep him off the drink. She's an attractive girl, a very nice girl, and a lot of men would leap at the chance to make it with her.'

Jennet was incensed by that arrogantly male attitude. 'Including yourself, I suppose?' she said tartly.

'Sure. Why not? I've a weakness for blondes,' Duncan drawled provocatively, with a flickering glance at the mass of fair hair piled high on the theatre sister's head, a bright aureole with the September sun behind.

Jennet scowled. 'She'd be safer with Paul! He's less likely to hurt her or her career than you are!' She didn't pause to analyse the spurt of anger or to wonder if he were really a man to take and break a woman's heart without conscience. *She* wouldn't trust him, she decided hotly. He was devastatingly attractive and extremely eligible—and still single. That last fact spoke volumes! 'I know your type,' she said scathingly. 'The one that gets away—time after time!'

Duncan was amused by the heat of indignation. She had reacted as he had hoped to that light praise of another woman and he was encouraged by the feminine spark of resentment. 'Is that how you see me? I wonder why.'

She flicked the still-loose button on his coat sleeve with a contemptuous finger. 'It's obvious that there's no permanent woman in *your* life or you wouldn't walk around like a ragbag.'

Duncan smiled. 'You're observant. No, there's no permanent woman in my life, as it happens. A *wife*, you mean, don't you? Don't be afraid to ask,' he said smoothly. 'It's no secret that I've never married. Ambition and that kind of commitment seldom go hand in hand for a surgeon, you know.' Only once had he been .torn between his work and a woman—and the latter had lost. But he had never felt so strongly or so surely about Christine as he felt about the proud and pretty theatre sister who looked at him as if she would like to see him lying dead at her feet.

Jennet was trembling. 'I doubt if you know

anything at all about "that kind of commitment".
Love, you mean, don't you? she retaliated, infuriated
by the gentle mockery of voice and smile.

Amusement lurked in deep-set grey eyes. 'Try me,
Sister . . .'

She was brought sharply to her senses by the
unmistakably sensuous invitation in the way he
leaned towards her, held her gaze, smiled into her
eyes. How stupid to bandy words with this
conceited charmer who thought he had only to
smile, to beckon, and any woman he fancied would
fall into his arms. How insane to be *tempted* for a
brief, breathless moment . . .

'Your interpretation of the word isn't likely to
agree with mine,' she said snubbingly.

'Know all about love, do you? Since you fell for
some guy in Greece?' Duncan shook his head in
wry reproach, and hummed a few bars of an old
tune at her. 'Know that one?' he asked, smiling. 'It's
old, but the truth of the lyrics is as new as ever. It
warns how easily fascination can be mistaken for
true love. Especially when you're lost in the magic
of a kiss.' He got to his feet. 'Think about it, Jennet.'

The velvet of his softened voice turned her name
into an endearment and brought a rush of colour
to her cheeks as he strode towards the door with a
dismissive set to his broad back.

Jennet looked after him with seesawing
emotions, torn between annoyance and
admiration. He was a challenge and a frustration,
an excitement and an exasperation, all at the same
time. Irritation won as she thought of the arrogance
of his unsolicited advice. She didn't need Duncan
Blair to point out that it was easy to mistake one's
feelings when mood and surroundings were

conducive to romance, she thought crossly.

She had yet to be convinced that she *had* made a mistake. Surely it was only natural to have some doubts . . .

As for that nonsense about Paul and Verity—well, it couldn't be anything else, Jennet decided as she went back to Theatres. The loss of Frida was surely too recent, too much mourned, for Paul to be seeking consolation in any woman's arms just yet. And was it likely that he would turn to someone as young and inexperienced and vulnerable as Verity when there were plenty of older women only too eager to take Frida's place in his life?

She couldn't believe that Paul would take advantage of a young girl's foolish attachment to her boss. It was easier to believe that Verity fancied herself in love, deceived by Paul's warm smiles, his soft words of encouragement, his kindly interest in her progress, into thinking that he cared for her. But it seemed that others were deceived, too, if Duncan Blair could be believed.

Were tongues wagging? Jennet wondered as she supervised the preparation of Theatre Three for a thoracotomy. If so, then Paul ought to be warned that his unthinking charm was misleading. Who better to slip a quiet word into his ear than herself?

As a rule, Jennet enjoyed working with Jamie Anderson, the good-natured thoracic surgeon from the Chest Unit who liked her to scrub for him whenever she was free, but she found her thoughts wandering that afternoon as she handed instruments and swabbed and threaded suture needles. Duncan Blair seemed to figure largely in her distraction. It would be easier to dismiss him if he weren't so attractive, she admitted, rejecting the disturbing image of the registrar's powerful frame, his rugged good looks and slow, stirring smile for perhaps the tenth time.

She was usually so level-headed about men, too. She was regarded by her colleagues at the Fitz as a coolly competent theatre sister with little time or taste for flirtation, but off duty she was warm and lively and sometimes impulsively encouraging, and would-be lovers were baffled by her stubborn virginity. She wasn't prudish or cold. It was just that she had never met a man who could move heaven and earth with a kiss.

It troubled her that Duncan Blair might have that shattering effect on her senses if she were foolish enough to walk into arms that seemed eager to hold her. There was a dangerous sensuality about the surgeon that struck an instant echo of response she had never suspected in herself. It was odd and unexpected and not at all welcome that a man she disliked and despised had the power to send those delicious shudders of delight through her at a touch, but there was no accounting for chemistry, she reminded herself sensibly. It was no more than a physical reaction to his male magnetism that would surely soon be crushed out of existence by the force of her contempt.

In the meantime it might be wise to avoid a man whose touch excited her more than she cared to admit . . .

Going off duty, she saw Verity, walking weary-footed and slump-shouldered across Main Hall, hands jammed into the pockets of her short, unbuttoned jacket, the chronic weariness of the overworked junior doctor stamped on her finely sculpted features.

With Duncan Blair's words echoing in her head, Jennet looked at her friend with new eyes. Tall and slender, with only the suggestion of breasts beneath the stylish grey suit and crisp white silk shirt, she contrived to seem alluringly feminine. Most men would admire the sparkling green eyes, the delicate colouring and pure bone structure of a lovely face, pale hair cut short to cling to her head in a cap of shining silk. Those cool good looks had attracted the registrar's interest. Why not Paul's, too?

He admired the Nordic type. Both her mother and Frida had been tall and slim and very blonde, Jennet reminded herself. Verity was a desirable woman with a youthful eagerness to please that had possibly already pleased a lonely widower, she told herself realistically. She might shrink from a vision of Paul and Verity as lovers, but she had to admit that it was a very real possibility.

Wrapped in her own thoughts, Verity almost walked past the theatre sister who waited for her by the heavy, plate-glass exit doors. She stopped short as Jennet spoke, blinking dreams from her eyes.

'Sorry! I didn't see you!' she apologised with a rueful smile. 'I'm almost asleep on my feet.'

'It shows,' Jennet teased warmly, smiling her sympathy. She *liked* Verity. They had become good friends in the last few months. Whatever the truth of her relationship with Paul, there was no reason why they shouldn't remain friends, she determined. 'Going home? I'll give you a lift . . .'

She knew that Verity couldn't afford to run even a small car, having mortgaged herself to the hilt to buy a small flat near the hospital. Like many newly

qualified doctors, she had been desperate to escape
the restrictions of residence. Jennet stifled the
thought that her friend might have been equally
anxious for the freedom to entertain an eminent
surgeon outside the hospital precincts.

'Thanks. That walk can be the last straw after a
long day,' Verity said gratefully, following Jennet
down the wide stone steps of the porticoed main
entrance, both girls dodging the steady stream of
people heading for the wards with the approach of
evening visiting hours. 'I didn't get much sleep last
night and I was on call at six this morning.' She
shot a sidelong glance at Jennet as she spoke.

Jennet didn't notice a certain constraint in
Verity's manner, busily hunting in her bag for keys
as they turned towards the staff car park. 'You're
off duty this weekend, aren't you? I expect you're
looking forward to the break.'

'Very much. Paul's told you, then?' There was a
hint of relief mingled with apprehension in her
tone.

Jennet's heart jumped. 'Told me . . .?' she echoed
casually, fumbling with the car keys, far from
anxious to hear what Verity was obviously itching
to impart and hoping against hope that it wasn't
confirmation of Duncan Blair's assertions.

'That we're going sailing this weekend. He's
taking me down to Chichester.' The defensive
breeziness of the words challenged Jennet to
disapprove.

'Oh, I see . . .' She didn't know what to say. The
boat had lain idle in Chichester Harbour since
Frida's death and it would be a sure sign of Paul's
recovery if he were to take it out to sea once more,
even with a most unsuitable companion. But she

was appalled by Verity's readiness to accompany him on a sailing trip.

'You spoke as if you knew.'

'No. I haven't seen Paul today.' Jennet doubted that he would have confided in her, in any case. He had probably hoped to slip away for a weekend with Verity without letting anyone know that he was being so indiscreet. 'It was a sudden decision, I take it?'

'Very. I meant to tell you earlier but things got in the way. I don't suppose you realised, but you did me a favour last night. Paul took *me* to Lester's as you were busy and we had a fabulous time.'

'How did that come about?' Jennet tried to sound merely interested rather than horrified as she slid behind the wheel of the Sierra.

'I said it was a pity to waste the reservation and it was my first night off in weeks and how would he like to help me celebrate. Shameless, aren't I?' There was a brittle quality to Verity's light laugh as she settled herself in the passenger seat next to Jennet. 'But it paid off. It was the best night of my life.'

'And how was he?' Jennet asked cautiously.

Verity fastened her seatbelt with careful concentration. 'Did he drink too much, do you mean? He drank enough to forget that he's twice my age and not so much that he couldn't perform,' she said deliberately.

'*Verity!*' Jennet was shocked by the airy triumph of the tone rather than the words and their implication, and she couldn't help a hint of old-fashioned disapproval from showing.

Verity coloured slightly even as she shrugged. 'Sorry. I know we're talking about your father, but he isn't *old* and you can't expect him to live like a monk for the rest of his life,' she muttered, resenting the censure that threatened to spoil a night to remember and cheapen something that only happened because she was deeply in love.

'I *don't*! Of course I don't! But——' Jennet broke off, reluctant to· hurt but convinced that Paul had taken advantage of Verity's infatuation for him because he had been drinking steadily throughout the evening that they had spent together. Stone-cold sober, he would never have been so foolish!

'But you didn't think he'd ever look twice at me. And if he took me to bed then it was only because I threw myself at him and he was sorry for me,' Verity suggested coldly.

'No! Nothing like that!' Jennet was hot with embarrassment. 'I'm sure that he finds you very attractive—I mean, you *are*!' And Paul wasn't the only man to notice, she thought, recalling the way that Duncan Blair had swept Verity from the unit with a smile that could charm birds from the trees. She marvelled that any girl could prefer a widower in his forties, with a drinking problem, to the attractive registrar. Paul had his own brand of charm, of course. But it was still astonishing that Verity had fallen for it so heavily.

'But you still don't understand it,' Verity said shrewdly.

Jennet stared through the windscreen at the jam of rush-hour traffic that held them up in the High Street. 'I don't think *you* understand,' she said quietly, troubled. 'Paul loved Frida very much. He went through all kinds of hell when she died, blaming himself for letting her take the car that night, feeling guilty because she stormed off in a temper and he hadn't tried to stop her although the weather was so foul. It's taking him a long time to get over her. Sometimes, I think he never will. He just doesn't see other women, Verity,' she persisted, doing her best to steer her friend away from inevitable heartache and disappointment. 'Only Frida . . .'

'He wasn't making love to Frida last night,' Verity maintained stubbornly.

Jennet winced. 'Then he was drunk,' she said harshly, cruel to be kind. 'Too drunk to know or care *who* he was holding in his arms.'

It was Verity's turn to wince.

Both girls were silent for the rest of the short drive. Jennet sighed as she overtook a bus to take a right turn into Verity's narrow road, feeling that she'd wasted her breath on a besotted girl who didn't want to accept that she was a temporary consolation for a man who had lost the wife he loved in tragic circumstances.

'Coming in for coffee?' Verity invited with slightly forced friendliness as the car came to a halt outside the big house which had been converted into cramped apartments. 'Or are you rushing off to meet Jeff?' She wished that she could rejoice for Jennet's obviously satisfactory romance with the American she had met on holiday. But the problems attached to her own love story were paramount at the moment.

'I am, actually . . .' Jennet was glad of a valid reason for refusing. She didn't want to hurt Verity's feelings but nor did she want it to seem that she condoned her friend's folly and Paul's indiscretion.

'I won't pry,' Verity teased. 'But I expect to be the

first to know when you get engaged! Come to
dinner one night next week. You *and* Paul, I
thought. Jeff, too, if you think he'd enjoy it.'

'I think he's the only one who would,' Jennet said
bluntly. 'It's an impossible situation, Verity. You
must see that.'

'I don't agree. Paul and are I free agents.'

'Free to hurt each other!'

Verity got out of the car. Pausing on the
pavement, she said simply. 'I love him. I know I
can make him happy. That's all that matters.'

'For how long?'

'As long as he needs me.'

'How long will that content *you*, I mean?' Jennet
knew a little about the longings, the impatience,
the hopes and dreams of a girl in love. 'I hate to
sound like an agony aunt but you'll want more than
he can give you, Verity. Or are you daft enough to
think he'll *marry* you?' she demanded in sudden,
appalled suspicion.

Verity smiled. 'Who knows?'

That confident little smile and the glow in her
friend's eyes haunted Jennet as she dressed to
spend the evening with Jeff. She felt uncomfortable
thinking of a sexual liaison between her father and
her friend, but it obviously existed, and she couldn't
help wondering if Verity was so good in bed that
Paul would want to pursue the affair to
extraordinary lengths—even to the point of
marriage with a girl half his age!

She'd had one stepmother. She didn't want
another! But if Paul had found something he really
wanted and needed in the seemingly unworldly
Verity . . .?

Oh, but it could only be the satisfaction of a

temporary physical urge on both sides, she comforted herself. Verity couldn't seriously be thinking of love and marriage in connection with a middle-aged widower who was the father of her best friend!

It was *sick*, Jennet thought crossly, as she hurried to open the door to Jeff, hardly knowing whether she most blamed Paul or Verity for such a stupid entanglement. Paul ought to know better. And Verity should have fallen for someone more suitable—someone like the registrar who so obviously admired her, for instance!

Jeff took her to a famous nightclub that was a favourite haunt of young royals and show-business celebrities. He was admiring and attentive and excellent company. They dined and danced and drank champagne and found so much to talk about that the evening sped on wings, but something was lacking in Jennet's enjoyment of those hours with the good-looking American.

Between them, Duncan Blair and Verity had cast a slight shadow on her mood, the surgeon by planting the seeds of suspicion and Verity by confirming that an affair with Paul was already in full flower.

Strangely enough, Jennet's disquiet seemed to be centred on Duncan Blair's obvious dislike of the situation between Verity and Paul. It wasn't possible that she was *jealous* of the registrar's interest in her friend, suspicious that it sprang from something more valuable and lasting than sex.

Or was it . . .?

CHAPTER SIX

LATHERING hands and arms and scrubbing them with meticulous care, Duncan studied the theatre sister's reflection in a mirror, a slender figure in green gown and mob cap, a few tendrils of bright hair escaping to curl on the back of a long, vulnerable neck. Her deft hands checked and re-checked instruments but her lovely head was probably full of romantic notions about a man whose very existence filled him with a fierce, black jealousy.

Grey eyes darkened with desire as he studied her. She was gorgeous, a lovely, lovely girl with a face that kept a man looking and longing and a body that triggered the kind of fantasies that had kept him awake well into the night and had haunted his dreams when he finally slept.

Every other woman paled into insignificance beside the beautiful Jennet Carter with her luminous skin and amber eyes and enchanting smile. Duncan knew he was in thrall to more than her bewitching loveliness, however. She was his woman, his destiny, his lasting passion. Having found her at last, all he had to do was to convince her that he was the man she wanted to be with for the rest of her life.

Not an easy achievement while the chunky American dominated her dreams, Duncan admitted wryly. He refused to accept that it smacked of the impossible . . .

'I could use a towel, Sister.' The thought of her in that other man's arms triggered the brusqueness of his tone.

Jennet turned, instantly incensed by his manner and thankful that no junior nurse was around to hear the arrant rudeness of the request. Most unusually, they were alone in the theatre suite, for he had arrived before anyone else, coming directly from the Cardiac Unit where he had been working since the early hours of the morning. Finding him there on her arrival, she had greeted him perfunctorily and begun the routine preparation of the theatre, doing her best to ignore the surgeon as he scrubbed.

His powerful frame filled the doorway that connected annexe with operating-room, arms held high and water dripping from his elbows, a gleam of impatience in grey eyes beneath imperious brows. Curt, unsmiling, arrogant—and the bane of her life since first meeting, Jennet thought wrathfully, wishing he had never come to the Fitz to disturb her peace of mind and stir her senses.

Seizing a pile of sterile towels in their plastic packs, she stalked towards the registrar. Without a word, she ripped open the top pack and offered the exposed towel, her expression cool and haughty and full of the dislike that vied so fiercely with unwilling desire.

Duncan reached for her instead, the packs scattering about their feet as he pulled her close, lowering his dark chestnut head to capture her sweet, startled mouth before she could utter a protest.

His embrace was just as powerful as Jennet had imagined—but it was more than the surgeon's strength that kept her captive. Her senses soaring as he kissed her, the length of his body pressed against her, she was all quick-fired longing, thrilling and throbbing and swept with the tumultuous wanting that he ignited at a touch.

It was a brief melting. Jennet wrenched herself out of his arms as the sound of voices out in the corridor announced the arrival of some of the theatre nurses. 'Don't ever do that again!' she stormed, low-voiced, so angry that she trembled from head to foot, eyes flashing amber fire.

Duncan was satisfied with the way her lips, cool at first, had warmed to his determined kiss and the way her body had yielded, albeit briefly, to the command in his embrace. She might dislike him as much as he probably deserved, but she wasn't immune to the physical power that had overwhelmed other women in the past—and that was surely a beginning. He wanted her to love him, but for the moment he would be content if he could persuade her to want him with an intensity of desire that matched his own for the stubborn theatre sister.

'I might,' he drawled provocatively, eyes dancing. 'Don't expect me to promise, Sister. You're very kissable.'

Jennet turned from the mocking humour in the grey eyes and the attractive quirk of his warm mouth, forced to conceal her fury and her self-disgust as nurses trooped in, noisy and exuberant and fortunately more concerned with themselves than with the tension between theatre sister and surgeon. But, to her overwrought sensitivity, it seemed to hover between them, and she hastened to dispel it with brisk, business-like efficiency.

'Would you pick up these packs and take them into the scrub annexe, please, Nurse Mills?' She found a bright smile for the junior nurse. 'I'm afraid I had a slight accident with them.'

'Sorry about that, Sister. Clumsy of me,' Duncan purred, taking blame so smoothly that it implied a minor collision in a doorway instead of the fusing of two bodies in urgent embrace.

Unappeased by what might or might not be an attempt at apology for forcing that kiss upon her, Jennet sent him a baleful glance and began to delegate jobs, splitting friends who might have their heads together in intimate gossip about boyfriends or the events of the previous evening or the odd behaviour of senior staff, pairing an experienced third-year with the apprehensive first-year doing her first stint in Theatres.

She was conscious of Duncan's amused study for a few moments. Then he began to chat up a staff nurse, who reacted with a girlishness most unsuited to her forty-odd years, in Jennet's critical view. He had the apparent ability to charm every woman from eight to eighty, she thought crossly.

She was furious with him, not only because he had taken advantage of the early hour and an empty theatre suite to seize and kiss her without warning, but also because he had undoubtedly known that his sexuality evoked instant response in her virtually unawakened self.

She was alarmed, too. For how *could* she want him, a man she disliked and despised and resented for a number of very good reasons? How *could* she yearn for a man she scarcely knew and ache to sink into the dark, fathomless depths of uncharted waters in his arms?

Her thoughts flew to Jeff. He was the kind of man she admired and trusted and had always dreamt of meeting and marrying one day. She knew where she stood with the gentle, easy-going, good-natured American who seemed content to wait until she was ready to give, and didn't demand her surrender with the insistent hunger in a kiss and the burn of desire in a touch.

Jennet was under no illusions where Duncan Blair was concerned. She knew just what he wanted from her and she had no intention of succumbing to a foolish, wanton response to an obvious and totally sexual interest.

Her refuge from the temptation in his smile, his dancing eyes, his velvet voice lay in Jeff's solid and reliable embrace. Jeff would love her and look after her and keep her safe from the lure of a man who obviously had no inclination for anything more than the heady delights of casual sex with any woman he fancied. There could be no joy and no future in loving a man like Duncan Blair, and Jennet was thankful that love played no part at all in the tumult of her emotions.

Love was what she felt for Jeff, she told herself sensibly, warming to the man who was courting her with tenderness and patience as well as ardour. Love was trust and respect and liking and being comfortable in a man's company. Love was the reward that Jeff had surely earned with his romantic pursuit of her, and Jennet impulsively decided that she *would* marry him and start a new life with him on the other side of the world.

Nursing had lost much of its attraction for her since she had been compelled to work in close proximity to her father's new registrar. Perhaps it had been *meant* that Jeff should come into her life at about the same time that Duncan Blair took up his appointment at the Fitz . . .

Theatre Three began to hum with activity and soon everything was ready for the first procedure of the day. The patient had been brought up from the ward and waited in the ante-room, drowsy from the pre-med and attended by a staff-nurse. Green-gowned surgeons, gloved and masked, talked in low tones as they waited for the consultant to arrive and scrub for surgery. Nurses had been primed in their duties and the anaesthetist had thoroughly checked the efficiency of his equipment. Other essential equipment had been supplied and set up by theatre technicians. A cluster of arc lights was positioned above the operating-area and a tray of instruments gleamed in their bright glow until Jennet covered them over with a sterile drape.

The theatre clock steadily ticked away the minutes and still there was no sign of Paul. 'Don't *you* know where he is, Verity?' Duncan flexed hands that were itching to begin work.

It was impatient, and so pointed that the young doctor looked daggers. 'I haven't seen him,' she said shortly, trying not to show her anxiety. A number of phone-calls to Paul's apartment had brought no response last night or this morning, and she had no idea if he was till taking her away that weekend.

'How about you, Sister?' The registrar turned to the girl who was calmly counting swabs as if she was unaware of his mounting exasperation with her absent father.

Jennet bridled at the belligerent tone. 'I expect

he's on his way,' she said briskly, resisting the
temptation to steal yet another anxious glance at
the clock. 'Any number of things may have delayed
him.'

'Damned man gets more and more unreliable,'
Duncan growled. 'We'll have the patient in and
make a start, anyway. No doubt your father will
stroll in just as I'm tying the last suture and proceed
to take all the credit for another Carter success!'

Jennet flushed with annoyance, but she let the
offensive words pass without comment. Paul *was*
becoming unreliable, and it was impossible not to
sympathise to some extent with the registrar who
had to cope with the extra work as well as make
the life-or-death decisions that were the
responsibility of a consultant. The game without
the name, he must feel at times, standing in for a
man who was neither old nor ill but apparently
just indifferent to the consequences of his erratic
behaviour.

Paul was very late. Apparently there had been
occasions during her holiday when he hadn't
turned up at all for listed surgery or to take a clinic,
and she was troubled. She had tried to contact him
but he was either not answering his telephone or
he had gone away without telling anyone.

It wasn't like him to put private patients or his
pleasure before the long-standing commitment to
the Fitz, but he had changed so much in the
months since Frida's death that Jennet felt she no
longer knew him very well. Drinking, womanising
and neglecting his work were all faults that she
didn't easily associate with her brilliant father, she
thought wryly.

He couldn't continue to delegate so much of his

work to a junior colleague without some comeback from the hospital authorities who contracted his services—and Duncan Blair was ready and waiting to step into his shoes. He seemed to have the necessary qualifications and experience, and he was exceptionally good at his job. If Paul didn't take care, he would be ousted from his post as senior consultant surgeon to the Cardiac Unit by an ambitious and very determined registrar!

Jennet shrank from tackling her father about his drinking problem as well as his unwise relationship with Verity, but *someone* had to be his conscience, she told herself resolutely as she let herself in to the luxurious penthouse apartment overlooking the river. Instead of driving straight home after leaving the hospital, she had decided to investigate Paul's failure to turn up for the day's list and the absence of any message from him.

It had been suggested that she should live with Paul and Frida when she first began her training at the Fitz, but Jennet had chosen to live in the Nurses' Home with the rest of her set. Later she had moved into the flat in Pilgrim House with a fellow third-year nurse. Paul had given her a key to the apartment, however, telling her to regard it as home.

Now she wondered if it would have helped if she had moved in with her father after Frida's sudden death. Such an arrangement might have been restricting and inhibiting to them both but at least she could have supervised the extent of his drinking and kept him out of the wrong arms!

Jennet walked into the living-room with its ultra-modern décor and furnishings, its valuable paintings and porcelain, its tall windows which

opened out to the glass-walled roof garden with the
unrivalled view of London's skyscrapers. The
afternoon sun glinted on the golden dome of St
Paul's and shimmered on the river that wound
through the city, spanned by London's many
famous bridges. She loved that view but now she
dismissed it with a cursory glance, shocked by the
chaotic state of the room.

Sofa cushions were disarranged and thrown to
the floor along with a trail of discarded clothing.
Shards of broken porcelain testified to the sweep
of a violent hand. A whisky bottle lay on its side
on a coffee-table, with some of its amber contents
still trickling steadily on to the thick carpet. A glass
had been smashed against a wall in a sudden act
of frustration or anger. Frida's portrait had been
turned face to the wall as if Paul could no longer
bear to look upon the cool, serene loveliness of the
wife he mourned.

The room still held a trace of Frida's favourite
perfume, and Jennet's spine prickled. How had
Paul endured coming home day after day to so
many reminders. It was scarcely surprising that he
had tried to forget through drink or in the arms of
another woman, she decided on a surge of
compassion.

She felt guilt, too. For she had let him down. She
hadn't fully understood his loneliness or his grief.
She hadn't always been there when needed. She
had believed his assurance that he was fine,
managing, getting over it and filling his life with
other things, and she had closed her eyes to his
increasing dependence on drink and its inevitable
effect on his work, his life, his relationships.

While Verity had seen and cared and done what

she could to comfort Paul—and *she* had absolutely no right to criticise or condemn, Jennet told herself sternly.

She scooped up a sofa cushion and then swung round, with it clutched to her breast. She had supposed Paul to be out or away and the apartment to be empty, but that had certainly been a sound from the direction of the kitchen.

'Is that you, Paul?' She took a step towards the open door as a shadow fell across the sunlit hallway dividing living-room and kitchen, and then caught her breath in surprise as Duncan Blair's broad frame filled the doorway. 'What are *you* doing here?' she demanded.

'Making coffee.' The registrar's grey eyes swept her with a glimmer of amusement in their depths. 'You won't need that for protection, Sister. Making love to you is the last thing on my mind just now. Later, perhaps . . .' he added provocatively.

'What . . .? *Oh!*' A blush swamped Jennet's expressive face at the mocking promise of the words. 'I might want it handy to throw at your arrogant head,' she said coldly. But she dropped the cushion on the sofa and then stalked past him and into the kitchen where the percolator bubbled busily and coffee-cups were set out on a tray. 'You're making this for Paul, I suppose? Where is he?'

'In the shower.' Duncan set a shoulder against the door-frame and folded his arms across his powerful chest, grey eyes regarding her intently. 'I had to use a certain amount of force to persuade him that it's time he sobered up. Being permanently drunk seems to appeal to him more at the moment. I found him slumped across his bed with a bottle of whisky at his side and I should think he's been drinking steadily for the past twenty-four hours.'

'How did you get in?' Jennet asked on a note of suspicion.

'Bribed the hall porter. He knows me from previous visits so it wasn't too difficult to get him to use his master key. You might have said that you meant to look in on Paul and saved me a tenner,' he reproached her.

'How was I to know that you intended to check up on him this afternoon? I didn't think that you were so concerned about him!' she countered.

'I've a lot of respect for your father,' Duncan said firmly. 'We're old friends.' He smiled slightly as he saw a sceptical gleam in her amber eyes. 'That surprises you, does it? Did it never occur to you that I get angry with Paul because I hate to see what's happening to him?'

'No,' Jennet returned bluntly and without hesitation, but a shade of doubt crossed her expressive face. It was a new slant—and it might even be true. She fancied that he was a man who hated compromise and insisted on integrity in people he cared about. He was harsh and demanding but he was probably a good and true friend who never let anyone down if he could help it, she decided, surprised to find herself looking for good in him.

The registrar shrugged. 'I've known and admired Paul since my medical-student days when he was generous with his time and his teaching.'

Her eyes narrowed. 'I wasn't aware that you *were* a medical student at the Fitz.'

He shook his head in mock despair. 'You haven't done your homework, Sister.'

'Perhaps I haven't been interested,' she said sharply.

'Well, it was long before your time,' Duncan conceded. 'Paul was senior registrar in those days and he taught me almost everything I know about technique. I leapt at the chance to work with him again. It was a blow to find him turning into an alcoholic—and even more of a blow to discover that his daughter doesn't care enough to do something about it,' he added deliberately.

'I *do* care.' Jennet said with an indignant glower. 'Did it never occur to you that I just don't know how to handle it?'

'You've never been very close, have you?'

'I'm very concerned about Paul!' She bristled at the implication that she was indifferent to her father.

'That isn't what I said.' Duncan realised that he'd touched on a sensitive spot. 'It probably isn't your fault, Jennet. Paul isn't much of a family man, I know,' he soothed. He had known the consultant for fifteen years, on and off, and it had come as a surprise to learn that he had a daughter from his first marriage.

'I didn't see much of him while I was growing up. He was always so busy—and then there was Frida . . .' Jennet broke off as Paul appeared, unshaven, dark hair damp and tousled, a towelling robe hastily swept about his spare frame. Having heard his daughter's voice, he had come to investigate her presence in the apartment.

Impulsively, Jennet went to him and put both arms about him in the most natural of loving gestures. Moved, a little uncomfortable, Paul held her, cheek pressed to the bright hair. 'I'm OK,' he reassured her. 'I'm fine . . .'

She leaned away to look up at him, studying the pallid, fine-drawn features, searching the rueful eyes, seeing the uneven throb of a pulse in the lean jaw. 'You haven't been fine for a long time. I should have seen that things were getting on top of you,' she mourned.

Paul shot a baleful glance at his registrar. 'What the devil have you been telling her, Duncan?'

'Your daughter's a big girl now, Paul. She can face up to the fact that you have a drink problem. If you're prepared to face it too then that's the first step towards fighting it,' Duncan said brusquely.

Paul sidestepped the issue. 'Do I smell coffee?' He put Jennet away from him and ran a hand over his face and hair, badly in need of a drink, sweating and shaking.

He gulped black coffee under the eye of his anxious daughter and concerned colleague. He obviously didn't want to be compelled to think about his work, his patients, the effect of his drinking on Jennet and friends and future.

CHAPTER SEVEN

JENNET went out to the roof-garden while her father shaved and dressed and his registrar ensured that he didn't reach for the whisky bottle while doing so. She had suggested to Paul that she should move in with him. He had vetoed it, gently but firmly. She had asked him to stay with her at Pilgrim House for a few weeks and he had smilingly refused. She had ventured a reference to Verity and the proposed weekend of sailing, and his face had darkened so ominously that she had hastily changed the subject.

Verity might believe that she and Paul had an ongoing relationship, but it seemed likely to Jennet that he regretted that impulsive lapse into intimacy with her friend.

Leaning against a window, she slid back one of the heavy glass panes to allow the warm September sun to fall on her upturned face. It was a golden autumn that year, with temperatures higher than they had been for much of the summer, bright sun sailing across clear blue skies to gild the rooftops and reflect in a thousand windows of the tall office blocks surrounding the ancient heart of the city. For a few moments, Jennet allowed the agitated concern for her father to slip away as her mind filled with the image of another man who seemed to have a number of different facets to his character and a disturbing impact on her life.

Real understanding and affection underlay the

harshness of Duncan Blair's approach to Paul's problems, she realised. He was brusque and commanding and even arrogant in view of her father's seniority and standing, but it was plain that his opinion was valued by the friend and consultant who regretted the lost respect of recent weeks. Duncan made no apology for slating Paul's stupidity or rebuking his failure to seek help before the craving for alcohol took over his life. At the same time, the younger man's concern was genuine and caring and practical as he outlined plans for Paul's future welfare and well-being.

He was a good friend, in fact, Jennet thought with a little twist of regret that he didn't regard her as worth more than a fleeting dart of desire. He seemed to think that she was a cold and unfeeling daughter to Paul, and she couldn't help feeling that his opinion might be justified to some extent. She had been too busy leading her own life, planning her holiday in Greece and dreaming about a possible future with Jeff on the other side of the world, to realise Paul's need for a sympathetic ear and a shoulder to lean on, she admitted wryly. She had supposed her brilliant father to be strong and self-sufficient and able to cope with the shock of sudden bereavement combined with guilt—and she had allowed his proud assurances and her own inadequacy to distance them at a time when he needed her most.

Verity had been more sensitive, more supportive, even if it had been silly of her to get so heavily involved . . .

Jennet turned as the registrar strolled out to join her in the spacious, glass-walled room with its fernery and creeping plants and troughs of exotic blooms that had once received so much of Frida's attention and now showed signs of neglect. 'How is he?'

'Bloody-minded,' Duncan said with feeling. 'He admits that he's unwell and needs to take a holiday but he declares that drink isn't the real problem. I suggested that he should contact Alcoholics Anonymous for help, but he insists that he hasn't reached that stage. We're going to have to do this between us, I guess.'

Jennet veiled eyes that might betray the absurd leap of her heart at that linking 'we'. 'Perhaps Verity is the problem,' she ventured. 'She seems to think that they have a serious relationship.' She paused, hesitating to betray her friend's hopes and dreams but feeling that they were possibly a clue to the hunted look in Paul's dark eyes. 'She's even hinting at marriage.'

'Then she's a fool.'

She looked at him beneath the sweep of long, gold-tipped lashes, detecting jealousy in the curt tone. With a strange pang, she wondered what it was about Verity that both Paul and his registrar were drawn to her. A hint of passion beneath a cool reserve, perhaps. Well, she could be just as passionate if the right man touched a chord of response in her nature—and Duncan Blair was that man if he but knew it. Perhaps it was just as well that he *didn't* . . .

'We don't know what Paul promised her,' she said doubtfully. 'He might have said *anything* after a few drinks.'

'Then that may be something else that we must put right,' Duncan said firmly.

Again, Jennet thrilled to that 'we' before she

remembered that the registrar's own plans for Verity's future were probably the real object of the exercise. She scolded herself fiercely for wanting to share anything at all with the arrogant, ambitious man who wouldn't allow anyone or anything to stand in his way.

'A woman in love isn't easily turned aside from what she wants,' she warned tartly, wondering just how he would go about steering Verity away from Paul's arms and into his own.

Amusement lurked in grey eyes as he looked down at her from his magnificent and sometimes overwhelming height. 'I'd forgotten that you're an authority on love,' he mocked gently. 'Perhaps you should give *me* a few lessons, Sister. How about now?' Strong hands spanned her narrow waist and he drew her flexibly against him with a sudden, sure movement.

As his lips claimed hers with a thrilling urgency, Jennet knew a dark, delicious delight that sent quivering arrows of wild desire to shatter her senses and bemuse her brain and hustle her heart nearer to loving this man. She was swept by the surprise assault and her own instincts into responding to the determined seeking of his mouth and the hard pressure of his powerful body. But only for a moment.

'Oh!' she gasped, thrusting him away with a surge of shock and fury. 'I told you not to do that!'

'And I said I wouldn't promise.' Duncan took her lovely, flushed face in both hands and looked deep into sparkling amber eyes, trying to convey the throb of unexpected love as much as the longing that consumed him. 'Stop fighting me, Jennet,' he murmured. 'You want me just as much as I want you.'

She might have surrendered to the prompt of her heart and the melt of her flesh if she hadn't known that his wanting bore no resemblance to the way she was beginning to feel about the registrar. Maybe he *did* want her but it was for all the wrong reasons, she thought fiercely, alarm bells of hurt and pride and common sense drowning the heartbeat that quickened at the warm look in his eyes and the caress of his enclosing hands.

'Not very original,' she said with a cool little smile, breaking away from his disturbing touch and nearness. 'That line is as old as the hills and I'm surprised that you thought I'd fall for it.'

'*Are* there any new words?' Duncan demanded with a hint of impatience. '*Want, need, love*—aren't they all as old as time and just as new as ever between lovers? What does it matter what words are used, anyway? How can a man describe the feelings that rush in and change everything when a certain woman walks into his life?'

He had never expected to know the cataclysmic assault of loving that turned day and night into a constant craving for sight and sound and scent and touch of the one woman he would want, need, love with all his being until the end of time.

The almost angry words seemed to convey the passion of a fierce sexual need rather than the promise of a tender, lasting love that included but transcended physical desire. That kind of love was the axis round which spun every woman's hopes and dreams, Jennet thought with a wistful pang. He made no secret of his motives for making such a strong play for her and it wasn't flattering to be wanted for only one thing!

'*Actions* speak louder than any words—and I'm not talking about grabbing a girl and kissing her whether she likes it or not!' she said crossly. 'I hate your arrogance!'

A wry smile tugged at Duncan's mouth. 'OK. You hate my arrogance and I understand your reasons. I won't grab you and kiss you again. I'll ask first—and then you can call me a wimp.'

She scowled. 'You *don't* understand. I don't like your attitude. You treat me like an *object*! I want a man to make me feel special, to take time to get to know me, to take me out to dinner or the theatre or for drives into the country, to find out my interests and meet my friends and become a part of my life before he rushes me into bed! You haven't the time for any of that!'

'Did I mention bed?' Duncan arched an amused eyebrow, but the light tone and his mocking expression concealed dismay that he had so completely failed to impress the depth and integrity of his feeling for her upon the lovely theatre sister.

'No! You talked round it, but we both know what you want from me! I'd admire you more if you came straight to the obvious point so I can say no loud and clear!' Jennet declared scathingly.

'Your negative attitude has been saying it all for you for days,' he said drily.

'Not very plainly, or it wouldn't take so long to get through to you!'

'Hope springs eternal . . .' Duncan smiled, but hope had been dealt a death blow and he wasn't sure that there was any point in trying to resuscitate it. Better to walk away and try to forget her, maybe. Jennet's heart and mind had been set against him from the very beginning, and he wondered how he had been fool enough to fall so deeply in love with a girl who was more than half-way to loving another man.

He hadn't imagined her sweet and seductive response. He had only made the mistake of attaching the wrong importance to the sensuality that stirred at his touch, his kiss, his urgent embrace. No doubt the American was just as successful in arousing her—and a damn sight more successful at climbing into her bed, he thought on a sudden, searing flame of jealous anger.

That virginal air was probably no more than a sweet deception bestowed on her by the gods to lure a man into the folly of loving . . .

Jennet disdained to answer. There was no doubt in her mind just *what* he had hoped—and he had been doomed to disappointment from the beginning. If she wasn't prepared to go to bed with Jeff until she was really sure that she loved him, then it was even less likely that she would surrender to Duncan Blair's sensual appeal. Sex for its own sake had never attracted her even before she had met and melted with reluctant desire for her father's new registrar, and sex without love was totally out of order as far as she was concerned.

He might have better luck with Verity if he waited for her to outgrow the foolish fascination for an older man, Jennet thought with a touch of uncharacteristic pettiness that she instantly regretted. Duncan Blair had a talent for bringing out the worst in her, she thought resentfully, stalking away from him in angry mood.

She stopped short on the threshold as Paul ushered Verity into the living-room, relieving her of a small suitcase. The young doctor looked coolly

elegant and supremely self-possessed as she smiled
at her middle-aged lover.

'I took you at your word, you see,' she was saying
in a voice made brittle by anxiety camouflaged by
a pretence of confidence. 'I hope the weekend's still
on?' She looked across the room to Jennet and,
behind her, the tall figure of the registrar, with a
hint of defiance in her attitude.

Released from the demands of her job for three
precious days and desperate to spend them with
the man she loved, Verity had hurried home to
pack and then taken a taxi to Paul's apartment.

Paul promptly made up his mind. A few days
away with Verity would help him unwind, for she
had a serenity that soothed and relaxed him. She
restored his confidence and renewed his youth, too,
if only temporarily, and he drank less in her
company.

Jennet didn't quite know how it happened that
she and Duncan were hustled from the apartment
to allow her father to throw some things into a case,
send round for the car and make a call to arrange
for the boat to be ready and provisioned in
Chichester Harbour when he arrived later that day
with Verity.

Paul oozed with charm and gratitude and a quiet
determination to have his own way as he assured
them both that he was fine, that he wouldn't
attempt to drive the car, that Verity would be safe
at sea with him and that they should go away and
enjoy their own few days of freedom from the Fitz
and forget all about him and his problems.

Jennet was slightly annoyed that her desire to
help had been brushed aside as soon as Verity
arrived on the scene—and then she told herself

fairly that her friend was possibly the one person who could bring Paul back from the brink of self-destruction. She had seen the change of mood, the squaring of his shoulders, the way he looked at Verity, and instantly felt happier about their relationship. She might not understand the attraction, but perhaps they needed each other in some way that she was unable to fathom.

What did *she* know about love, after all? Except that it threatened a girl's entire happiness and peace of mind if it centred on a man who cared more for the brief gratification of the senses than for the exchange of hearts in mutual, lasting love.

'Well, they deserve each other,' Duncan said in impatient dismissal as he walked Jennet to her parked car. He had done his best, but it was obvious that Paul neither wanted nor appreciated his advice. So that was where Jennet got her obstinate streak, he thought drily.

Maybe *he* was at fault. Maybe he should stand back and keep quiet and allow the people he cared about to fall into pits of their own making. Good intentions were too often misconstrued and resented. A confident and positive approach to the problems of friends or colleagues or patients too often led to accusations of arrogance. Well, he had washed his hands of Paul and Verity. But Jennet was a different matter.

Jennet was too dear, too precious, and he still had to do what he could to protect her from grief. Duncan didn't know why he distrusted the American so much. It was a gut feeling, more than jealousy, although that certainly played some part in his attitude. Somehow he was sure that Jennet would come to harm at the man's hands unless she was surrounded by his love and kept safe by his vigilance.

If only she would let him get close to her, allow him, through friendship at least, the right to vet the man and his motives, to give himself a chance to prove that her true happiness lay with a man from her own world rather than with a stranger whom she had met in Greece.

But the beautiful theatre sister was as stubborn and as bloody-minded at times as her brilliant father . . .

'What are your plans?' Duncan rested a hand on the roof of the Sierra as Jennet produced keys and opened the car door. His own car was parked some way down the street.

'For Paul? None, now,' Jennet said briskly, having resigned herself to the fact that there was nothing she could do about the situation. Both Paul and Verity were consenting adults, after all. 'I suppose he's old enough to lead his own life,' she added with a wry smile.

'I've lost interest in your father for the moment, Jennet. I'm talking about us. Paul said we were to forget him and enjoy the weekend. Well, the weekend starts here, doesn't it? I can't offer you anything so exciting as a sail on the high seas, but I can promise to give you a wonderful evening.' Warm persuasion drawled in his deep voice.

'Me and you!' Startled, Jennet looked up at the registrar with a flutter of thick lashes and the hated tide of colour creeping into her cheeks.

'Me and you sounds about right,' Duncan agreed with a twinkle in grey eyes. 'I thought dinner and then a show . . .'

'As a prelude to bed, I suppose?' She crushed him

with the sweetness of her tone and the sparkle of militancy in her amber eyes. 'I think you must have got the wrong message, Mr Blair!' He had totally misunderstood her, she thought angrily, and now he was sure that he had only to change his approach and she would be persuaded to give him what he wanted.

Duncan arched an eyebrow. 'You said you wanted to be courted. Well, I'm courting,' he protested lightly.

'Don't be so ridiculous!' Jennet said sharply while her foolish heart turned somersaults at the mere thought of being wooed with serious intent by this most attractive of men.

Foolish heart, indeed, to feel that good looks and physical magnetism and smiling charm counted for more than the love and loyalty that Jeff offered her and would surely provide for the rest of their lives together!

'You're beautiful.' Duncan leaned to kiss her, warm mouth sliding with infinite tenderness over soft lips.

Jennet backed away. '*Don't!*'

Don't steal my heart and make it quite impossible for me to love Jeff or any other man, she meant. Don't melt my very bones with desire so deep, so consuming, that I can never wholeheartedly respond to Jeff or any other man for as long as I live.

He looked down at her, only a tautness of cheek muscles betraying the flame of mingled passion and anger that she continued to doubt and reject him so obstinately.

'Because I didn't ask?' he mocked gently. 'I've never asked in my life, Jennet.'

'Just taken it for granted that every woman you meet must fancy you! Well, this woman *doesn't* and I wish you'd leave me alone—and surely that must be plain enough even for you!' She whipped him with forced contempt in eyes and voice and trembling body, steeling herself against the charm and attraction of the clever, confident man with his air of never having been denied anything he wanted.

Her mouth still tingled from that butterfly kiss. Her heart banged about in her breast as if it sought to break its bounds and fly into his keeping. Her legs were weak and shook, and she was feeling quite sick with the passion of inexplicable emotions and torments. But she *wouldn't* give in to the irresistible tug of heart and body. She *wouldn't* be just another conquest for a sensual surgeon who seemed to have no heart to give in exchange for her own.

Besides, there was Jeff, and she had made up her mind to marry him, she reminded herself sternly. Whatever she felt for Duncan Blair, that strange confusion of sensations that swept her entire being whenever he was near, it certainly wasn't love! It was much more likely to be fascination—and hadn't the surgeon himself warned her against confusing the two?

'It could have been a night to remember, Jennet . . .' With a mock-sorrowful shake of his head, Duncan turned and strolled towards his prowl-nosed Jaguar, conceding defeat but only for the moment. A man who loved as deeply as he did wasn't likely to accept dismissal at first, second or even third telling.

Jennet was torn between a feeling of relief and

a rush of impulse to hurry after him and exclaim that she had changed her mind and she'd love to have dinner with him.

But shyness, a fear of making a fool of herself and the thought of Jeff combined to nail her feet firmly to the ground, and after that momentary hesitation she got into the car and switched on the engine.

It *would* be a night to remember, for the rest of her life, she thought defiantly, driving past the still-parked but purring Jaguar without a glance, heading for home and a leisurely hour or two getting ready to spend the evening with Jeff.

Out of the blue, he had come up with tickets almost impossible to obtain for the first night of a new Andrew Lloyd Webber musical. It was sure to be a thrilling and exciting experience, wonderful prelude to a glorious finale when she told Jeff that she would marry him.

After the show, he would take her to dine and dance at a West End club, and be her attentive escort, amusing companion—*and* perfect lover, she told herself firmly, sure that she would warm to him, well with the familiar affection for him and want to make him happy.

She might tell him over a glass of wine. She might whisper it in his ear as they danced, moving in locked embrace to the slow, romantic rhythm of the music. Or she might wait until he took her home, telling him to pay off the taxi and inviting him into the flat, where they would talk love and marriage and happy ever after before she finally went into arms that had ached to sweep her into the wonderful world of lovers ever since they had met on that beautiful Greek island . . .

CHAPTER EIGHT

SITTING beside Jeff in the darkened theatre, listening to the soar and swell of magical music and sensing the certainty of yet another runaway success for the brilliant composer who had cast his talented wife in this latest production, Jennet found it hard to concentrate on the spectacle unfolding on stage although she knew it must have cost Jeff a small fortune to secure their seats in the stalls.

Her thoughts kept turning to Paul and Verity, probably aboard the *Viking* and lost in their own private world at that hour. A case of the world well lost for love, she thought with an odd pang of envy—odd because wasn't *she* preparing to give up everything she knew and cared about to live in America with a man she really didn't know very well?

Duncan Blair's warnings kept coming to mind, too, only to be brushed away with impatience. *He* wanted her to break with Jeff so that he could step into his shoes. How astonished he would be to learn that she had never slept with Jeff or any other man! He thought she was any man's just for the asking—or *not* asking, in his case, she thought bitterly.

'Something on your mind, honey?' As the curtain came down with only the final act to follow, Jeff turned to her and brushed aside the clustering curls at her ear to slide his lips lazily across her cheek, a smile in his eyes. 'What's wrong? You don't seem to be enjoying the show.'

So he had sensed that she was slightly remote

from him and her surroundings at moments. Jennet hastened to make amends. 'I do! I love it! Such lovely songs, and the costumes and settings are magnificent,' she enthused. 'But it was sold out weeks ago, Jeff! How *did* you manage to get tickets at such short notice?'

Smiling, he laid a finger along the side of his nose in an age-old gesture. 'Someone owed me a favour.'

Jennet didn't doubt it. He seemed to have a number of contacts in most countries who could supply him with anything he wanted. Meeting him in Greece, she had thought him just another American businessman on holiday, generous, fun-loving, attractive and amusing but easily forgotten when their ways eventually parted. She had since learnt that there was more to Jefferson B. Lloyd than she had imagined as they swam and sunbathed and danced the night away together.

She had expected him to forget her very quickly, too. So it was puzzling if immensely flattering that a man with so much money and influence should be so interested in a very ordinary English nurse, although she shrewdly suspected that she had maintained some of that interest by keeping him at bay in a way that perhaps no other woman had done in the past.

Jeff probably thought it was feminine strategy to ensure that he put a wedding ring on her finger. In fact, it was simply a matter of chemistry . . .

As the lights went up on the first-nighters in their dinner jackets and elegant gowns and furs and glittering jewels, Jennet felt somewhat out of place in that glamorous gathering in the simple cream lace dress that had been an impulsive buy in Greece. But the warmth in Jeff's eyes assured her that she was admired and desired and she felt a very feminine glow.

He left her to make a telephone call and Jennet looked about her with interest, recognising a celebrated actor with his family, a famous novelist with her current escort, one or two politicians, the lead singer of a well-known group and a junior member of the Royal Family.

She turned in her seat to see if Jeff was on his way back as the orchestra struck up a reprise of an earlier number to warn the audience that the curtain would soon be raised. Across the aisle and some rows back, a man's rich chestnut head gleamed in the auditorium lighting, giving her a momentary shock. She hastily faced the stage once more, heart on the leap. But Duncan Blair was not the only man in the world with hair of that rich red-brown, and it was most unlikely that he sat behind them in the theatre that evening. She refused to stretch coincidence so far, Jennet told herself firmly.

She couldn't turn around for a better look. It might just be the registrar and she might just catch his eye, and that would be highly embarrassing!

Jeff resumed his seat at the end of the row, smiling in slightly absent apology. 'Sorry, honey. I've had trouble getting hold of this guy because of the time difference. This was the best time to call him.'

'Oh, I didn't mind being left on my own. I've been picking out famous faces,' she assured him, slipping a hand into his arm. The hum of expectancy in the theatre was infectious and she felt in holiday mood all over again, and this was the man with whom she had shared some magical moments in Greece. Rejecting the fleeting image of another man who had touched her with a different kind of magic, Jennet felt a rush of impulsive affection for the man at her side. Leaning towards him, she touched his cheek lightly with her lips. 'It's a wonderful evening, Jeff. I could get used to being spoilt in this way.'

'Marry me and I'll spoil you for the rest of your life,' Jeff said lightly.

'I might just do that.' There was a subtle promise in her shining eyes.

Jennet was totally unprepared for the violence of his reaction. Jeff reared instantly to his feet, dragging her with him. 'Let's get out of here! Why are we wasting time on a goddammed musical when I could be making love to you? Hell, honey, I want you so badly that I *ache*!'

He hustled her down the aisle with the grip of his hand crushing the fragile bones of her slender wrist. Wincing, too startled to protest, Jennet stumbled along at his side, clutching bag and coat and enormous box of chocolates and feeling that everyone was staring.

In fact, few heads turned. Most people were watching the slow rise of the curtain that revealed yet another and even more spectacular stage set. Jennet looked over her shoulder in response to the ripple of delighted applause but Jeff swept her from the auditorium with single-minded determination.

Her high heel turned on the wide, thickly carpeted steps and she almost lost her balance. 'Jeff! This is crazy! I want to see the end of the show,' she wailed.

He ignored the protest. 'Wait for me here while I hunt down a cab, honey . . .'

Abruptly abandoned in the almost deserted foyer, Jennet wondered if he planned to bundle her into a taxi and whisk her off to his hotel-room or her flat and into bed before she could draw breath—and if she would let it happen in spite of her earlier decision to celebrate their engagement in a way that would please and delight him.

Her spine pricked with sudden alarm at the thought that his unexpectedly masterful manner might sweep aside any last-minute change of mind on her part.

'You look as if you need rescuing, Sister.'

The deep, familiar voice reached out to her like a lifeline. Jennet turned to stare at the tall man in immaculate evening clothes who smiled at her with such devastating charm that her heart turned over and her legs turned to jelly.

'Oh, hello . . . no, I'm fine, thanks. I'm with someone . . .' She was anxious not to seem welcoming and cross with herself for that instinctive and utterly absurd reaction.

'The invisible man, presumably?' Duncan suggested drily.

Jennet didn't smile. 'Jeff will be back soon.' She looked anxiously towards the heavy outer doors, reluctant to be the object of the registrar's concern even for a moment. She needed to be rescued from *him*, she thought ruefully, flustered by the encounter and wondering how he contrived to appear at the most unexpected moments like some demon prince in a pantomime!

The swift come and go of colour in her lovely face and the betraying quiver of her sweet mouth caused a stir of love and longing in Duncan's breast. She was beautiful, so vulnerable and so impulsive that he feared for her and felt he would lay down his life to keep her from harm, although he had never seen himself in the role of knight on a white charger. It seemed that Jennet evoked a chivalry that didn't appear out of place even in these days of equality of the sexes, he thought tenderly.

'I saw you heading for the exit, getting out before the crush,' he said smoothly, giving her time to regain her composure. 'It seemed sensible to do the same. I'll catch the last act another time. This show will run for ever, of course. Another triumph for the Lloyd Webbers.'

'It's a wonderful show,' Jennet agreed, cheeks cooling as her heart steadied and her legs returned to normal. 'I loved it.'

'Then you'll want to see it again, if only for the really spectacular finale. Why not with me? I have a cousin in the cast who'll let me have a couple of seats whenever I want them.'

Her face lightened at the revealing words. 'So that's how you happen to be here this evening,' she said, rather unwisely.

Duncan's smile deepened and danced in his grey eyes, warming the craggy good looks. 'Did you think it was destiny? I'm afraid it was only coincidence.'

Jennet felt the blush surging to the very roots of her hair. 'I didn't think it was anything else!' she said sharply.

She walked away from him towards the street. Outside the famous theatre, she scanned the pavement for some sign of Jeff, baffled by his long absence. But it was like him to scour the neighbourhood instead of waiting for a cruising taxi to come along, she thought with some impatience. In fact, it was strange that he relied so heavily on taxis. A man in his position might be expected to have a chauffeur-driven car at his command.

Duncan put a light hand on her shoulder. 'Something seems to have happened to your friend, Jennet.'

At his touch, she felt a tingling shock that lifted the fine hair on her head and crept all the way down her spine to the very tip of her toes. It was an odd and alarming sensation, something she had read about but never really believed, and she didn't quite accept that it was actually happening to her. A kind of electricity had passed between them at that moment of physical contact. Surely Duncan had felt it, too! She didn't dare to turn, to look at him, afraid of what she might see in his eyes and what she might betray with her own.

'He's trying to get a taxi,' she said stiffly, defending Jeff although she was a little annoyed with him.

'It will be a minor miracle if he finds one free. All the theatres turn out at about this time.' Duncan's hand fell back to his side. The nearness of her, the sweet scent of her hair and the swirl of cream lace about that perfect figure kindled such a torment of longing in him that he felt it must communicate itself through his touch. Jennet had made it plain that it was unacceptable to her but still he persisted. He smiled down at her warmly. 'I can look after you better than this,' he said firmly. 'There'll be a party backstage after the show. Why not come along and meet my cousin Flora and the rest of the cast and let me run you home later? My car is parked behind the theatre.'

A party where the Lloyd Webbers were sure to be present! A chance to meet the charismatic couple and share in their triumph after the magnificent first night of a show that the critics must applaud! Jennet's heart bounded with delight and then sank as she realised that the invitation excluded Jeff as a matter of course. She *couldn't* accept!

A taxi drew up alongside them and Jeff leapt down to the pavement, casting a dourly suspicious glance at the man who stood beside Jennet. She turned to the registrar, her bright smile veiling disappointment.

'As you see, Jeff's a dab hand at miracles,' she said with a brittle gaiety that convinced Duncan of her preference for the American's charms and company. 'The party sounds fun but we've other plans . . .'

As Jeff swept her towards the taxi with a proprietorial grasp of an elbow, Jennet wondered wryly why *his* touch didn't have a similar shattering effect on her emotions.

Glancing back, she saw Duncan standing where they had left him, looking after the departing taxi with an inscrutable expression. Then he turned with a shrug of those broad shoulders and went back into the theatre.

She felt an odd tugging at her heart, a foolish inclination to stop the taxi and jump out and rush back to the man who tempted her to forget loyalty and common sense and everything else in his arms.

Jeff put an arm about her as they sat in the back of the taxi. 'Honey, I've arranged to be dropped off at the Hilton and then the cab will take you on to North London,' he said unexpectedly. 'That guy I called . . . well, he's going to ring me back and I gave him the number of the hotel. I've a feeling that this problem we have may take best part of the night to solve and involve me in a trip to Liverpool.'

'But—I don't understand . . . you said . . .' Jennet broke off, bewildered. Was this the same man who had been so apparently urgent to hustle her into bed? Or had that been merely a ruse to rush her from the theatre so that he could get back to his hotel in time for an expected telephone call?

She knew that he was unpredictable. Was it possible that he was also unreliable and manipulative? For the first time she felt distrust of his smooth charm and glib tongue and she wondered if he really meant any of the things he said and the promises he made, or if he had only sought her out to keep him company in occasional moments of leisure because he was the kind of man who couldn't do without female flattery. For all his protestations of love, she suddenly felt that she came a poor second to the business interests that had brought him to England so soon after they had met on holiday.

'I know how you feel, honey—and I hate to do this to you, believe me!' Jeff smiled into sceptical eyes. 'You know there's nothing I want more than to be with you, sweetheart. But I *am* supposed to be over here on business as much as pleasure, and something's come up that ought to be dealt with right away. I was tempted to ignore it for a few days—and who could blame me when *you're* the temptation? But I really owe it to my old man to make sure this deal goes through, and it's important that we keep him happy if I'm going to take you back to Washington as my wife.'

Jennet was tempted to tell him that such a prospect was becoming more unlikely by the moment and to remind him that he had assured her that his marriage to an English girl would delight his father. Instead, she swallowed chagrin and bit back a reproach, although it was infuriating to be tamely on her way home when she might have seen the end of the show *and* enjoyed a backstage party. Why on earth hadn't he explained earlier? Then she could have accepted Duncan's exciting invitation.

Jeff was full of surprises and not all of them were pleasant, she thought wryly, unconvinced by his explanation for the sudden change of plan. Then, with a welling of relief, she realised that it was a reprieve, whatever the reason was for his change of mind and mood. Now there was no likelihood at all that she would end the evening in bed with him. Or engaged to him.

Jennet sat back with his possessive arm about her and his unwanted kiss on her hair and wondered how she could have confused liking and loving to such an extent. She really had no desire to become Mrs Jefferson B. Lloyd and begin a new life on the other side of the Atlantic. She was perfectly happy as Theatre Sister Jennet Carter and she couldn't see herself rushing to marry any man. Not even one who moved her as surely and as strangely as Duncan Blair.

As the taxi carried her inexorably homewards and further from the glittering delights with which he had tempted her, Jennet tried not to feel cheated because Cinderella had been denied the chance of going to the ball on the arm of a very attractive Prince Charming. No doubt it was just as well, she told herself firmly. For she might have lost more than a glass slipper . . .

The weekend was a wash-out as far as Jennet was concerned. Jeff telephoned as he was leaving for Liverpool, telling her that he would be gone for a few days and assuring her that he would be in touch again as soon as he had returned to London. Jennet almost felt that she wouldn't care if she never saw him again, but resisted the impulse to tell him so, reluctant to seem petulant and not wanting him to suppose that she minded because he chose to put business before herself.

The weather was glorious, warm and sunny, perfect for sailing, and she felt quite envious of Verity on board the *Viking* with the man she loved. In different circumstances she might have driven down to Hampshire to join her father and her friend, but she knew she would be distinctly *de trop* that weekend.

Other friends were on duty or heavily involved in various social activities. Having expected to spend much of her time with Jeff, Jennet had made no other plans for the weekend and now found that she had little heart for anything.

She toyed with the idea of going to Wales, to see her grandmother, but dismissed it as impractical at short notice. Instead, she caught up with the housework and did some necessary shopping and paid a visit to the local launderette. For much of the weekend, she wandered aimlessly about the flat, switching on and switching off the television, uninterested in the radio, trying to read but soon bored with her book, trying to write long-overdue letters but unable to concentrate and constantly hovering near the telephone as if she half-hoped that Duncan would ring with another invitation. And perhaps she did.

But he didn't.

By Monday morning, Jennet went eagerly back to Theatre and the work she loved and found so satisfying. It had been a boring and lonely and rather depressing weekend. Her own company had always been sufficient for her in the past, sometimes very welcome after a demanding few days in Theatres, but now it gave her too much time to think. Her thoughts had led her down some unlikely avenues but always back to the tall, impressive figure of Duncan Blair as he stood silhouetted against the bright lighting of the theatre foyer.

Each time, she had felt again the shock of finality in the way that the registrar had turned, shrugged, dismissed her as she drove off in the taxi with Jeff.

But how could she blame him if he had decided to drop out of the apparent race to win her? A proud man didn't persist in his pursuit when a woman made it abundantly plain that she wasn't interested.

It would be foolish and dangerous to fancy that she had really hurt and disappointed him . . .

Jennet was caught unawares by the sudden, cramping contraction of her heart and then its flying leap as Duncan strolled into the scrub annexe, cap crammed over burnished hair and thin tunic stretched taut across his powerful chest.

She rushed into speech to drown the thumping of her heart and conceal the impact on her emotions that left her breathless and startled and wondering. 'Hello! How was the party? The reviews were marvellous, weren't they? Flora Singleton—is that your cousin? I see that she had a special mention.'

'I haven't read the reviews.' It was curt reply and there was no hint of warmth or friendliness in glance or manner as he strode to a basin and turned faucets and began to scrub.

The shine in those amber eyes, the warm curve to her mouth, the ill-concealed excitement in her voice and the heightened colour in her lovely face all hinted at a well-spent weekend. It seemed to

Duncan's jealous eyes that she *glowed* with all the radiance of a woman come newly from a lover's arms.

Having spent most of *his* weekend tortured by thought of the woman he loved, and passionately wanted, in the arms of another man, he was seized by a terrible, primitive urge to get hold of the American and tear him limb from limb. Then, having gained some small degree of satisfaction from the destruction of his rival, he would probably drag Jennet off by her glorious hair and make love to her with a savagery that would teach her not to wreak havoc in a man's life with her golden beauty and shimmering smile.

Jennet stared at the registrar's broad back, his deliberately averted head, hurt but even more annoyed by the snub. She fumed at her folly in offering an olive branch to the man who had swept it aside with his usual infuriating arrogance. She had exposed herself to the brusque and chilly indifference of a man who had obviously lost all interest in her.

No doubt he had found someone among the bevy of glamorous women at that backstage party to console him for a rejected invitation. Something twisted in her breast at the thought of other women enjoying his ardent lovemaking, melting in the white-hot flare of his passion.

Duncan Blair was sheer animal magnetism, and the danger lay in her instinctive response to his sensuality, Jennet warned herself sternly, hurrying to set her nurses to work as other surgeons arrived to scrub for the first procedure.

If she were as close to loving such a man as she feared, then now would be the time to rein in her flyaway heart . . .

CHAPTER NINE

SETTING out packs of sterile hypodermic syringes together with ampoules of the drugs that might be needed, Jennet turned with an angry sparkle in her eyes that faded as she realised that it was Paul's arm about her waist and Paul's lips that had aimed a light kiss at her green-masked cheek.

She would have been furious if it had been Duncan, making a most unethical pass at her in full view of everyone in the operating theatre. She would also have been secretly delighted by a softening of the harsh attitude he had suddenly adopted towards her.

'Thank goodness you're here!' She was relieved that her father had arrived in good time to scrub up. Another day or two on the *Viking* might have benefited him, but she had been dreading having to assist a coldly scornful registrar with the list that morning. 'And how well you look!' Tanned by the sea air and the sunshine of the brief heatwave, the whiter crinkles about Paul's dark eyes showed that he had laughed a lot in Verity's company.

'We were certainly fortunate in the weather,' he said as if that was all they had needed to make everything perfect.

'Enjoy the weekend?' Unnecessary question, she knew, seeing the new vitality in his handsome face and noting the new buoyancy of his mood.

'Very much. Verity's a great girl.' A number of fond memories softened his expression as he spoke.

'*Girl* is apt.' Jennet couldn't resist the slightly tart reminder.

Paul frowned. 'I know all the arguments, Jennet. Do you think I haven't tortured myself with them for weeks? I didn't just rush in and grab what Verity was offering, you know. Give me credit for some principles!' There was a flash of the quick, fierce temper so like Jennet's own in the low, taut words.

'I'm sorry . . . I've no right . . . I just want you to be happy . . .' Trying to make amends, she floundered badly, realising that she had underestimated the extent of his feeling for Verity and his personal struggle to combat it.

The flare of anger died. 'I know you do, sweetheart. And, like a good friend, you're worried about the effect of all this on Verity, I expect. We've talked a lot in the last few days, but I promise you that any decisions we make will be the best for Verity. She has the makings of a fine surgeon and I don't want to jeopardise her future in any way. I don't want to give her up, either,' Paul added with wry honesty.

He turned with a youthful eagerness that emphasised the last words as Verity came into the room. She was talking to Duncan but her glance skated swiftly, lovingly, towards Paul.

It was the merest exchange of meaningful looks but the remembrance of shared intimacy seemed to hover between them like a tangible cloud. They were so obviously lovers who didn't care if the whole world knew it that Jennet felt a stab of envy. It might seem an unlikely match, but perhaps Paul wasn't too old or Verity too young for them to find a lasting happiness with each other.

She was prepared to give them her blessing,

anyway . . .

Paul and Verity scrubbed together, side by side at basins as they went through the ritual with meticulous thoroughness, discussing procedure like equals rather than senior consultant surgeon and very junior doctor. Jennet envied her friend's easy confidence, too. Verity had known what she wanted and gone after it without fear of rebuff or failure.

She was more cautious. Be careful what you set your heart on, for you will surely attain it, ran an old Chinese proverb. She had set her heart on being a nurse, like her mother and like so many of the women in her father's world, and she had achieved that ambition. She had set her heart on becoming a theatre sister so that she could work with her father and earn his admiring approval, and it had eventually come about. She had set her heart on a holiday in Greece that summer, half hoping to find romance, and it had happened. Supposing she set her heart on a future with Duncan . . .?

Jennet shied away from such a foolish dream, sure it was doomed to disappointment. Having seen the tenderness in the grey eyes resting on her friend as Verity scrubbed and chatted to Paul, she knew that the registrar's feeling for the young doctor was unchanged by her involvement with another man. Perhaps he hoped that she would soon tire of Paul and turn to him. Perhaps, like Verity, he meant to work at turning a dream into reality instead of waiting and hoping for it to come true.

Jennet just didn't have that kind of confidence. After all, Duncan had never encouraged her to believe that he was offering more than a brief, passionate idyll, and it would be a terrible mistake to lose her heart to him.

It might be a very good idea for her to stop dreaming absurdly romantic dreams and concentrate on her work as a theatre sister, she told herself firmly.

'We have here a patient with severe mitral stenosis and I am about to perform a valvotomy to increase the lumen of the fibrosed valve,' Paul began formally as the theatre team gathered about the draped patient.

He was using an opportunity to turn a simple procedure into a teaching session for the junior surgeons in the operating theatre and the medical students who had crowded into the viewing gallery.

He was more relaxed than Jennet had seen him for some time as he began the procedure with a sure stroke of the scalpel. She wondered if Verity's presence at the Fitz and the growing torment of a desire he felt he must suppress had affected Paul's work even more than the steadily increasing intake of alcohol.

Watching the seemingly nerveless hands as they worked with restored confidence and familiar skill, listening as Paul outlined each step of the procedure for the benefit of the listening students, she was ready with each instrument as it was required and, as usual, the father-daughter relationship was forgotten in her desire to win the accolade of the brilliant surgeon's approval.

Absorbed in her work, she was able to ignore the tall registrar at her father's right hand except when she had to pass an artery clamp or retractor to him, and then she was careful not to meet the cool challenge of his grey eyes.

At some stage during the lengthy, complex

operation, Jennet had the feeling that she was standing outside herself, looking down on the green-clad group beneath the cluster of brilliant arc lights that bore down on the draped and unconscious patient. It was a familiar tableau of surgeons and theatre staff and a complicated array of equipment and machinery but it wasn't the hushed drama depicted by so many films and books.

There was a lot of lively conversation between Paul and his team, some teasing of Verity's slightly nervous assistance at one point, and a mild flirtation between Tim Gowan and one of the theatre nurses that Jennet knew she should nip in the bud. In no mood to play the role of martinet, she turned a blind eye and a deaf ear to their exchanges, although a busy operating theatre was no place for actual or would-be lovers to indulge in meaningful looks and murmurs.

Poor prognosis for any patient if a surgeon should be distracted by a girl he fancied in the midst of excising disease or repairing damaged nerves and tissues or exchanging new organs for old!

Jennet thought wryly that she wouldn't much mind swapping her heart for one that didn't behave so oddly whenever an ambitious, arrogant and much too attractive registrar was around.

At the end of the first procedure, the surgical team took a break. On his way from the theatre, Duncan walked past Jennet as if she simply didn't exist for him, and she felt that second snub like a physical blow, her heart plummeting like a stone. His attitude hurt more than it ought if she was only teetering on the verge of caring for him, and she feared that she had tumbled over the edge into loving at some moment when she wasn't watching her step.

But it seemed that she had rebuffed him once too often, and he wasn't prepared to forgive and forget this time. So there was nothing to do but pick herself up, dust herself down and get on with her busy, fulfilling and satisfying life as a theatre sister. She must forget all about the wistful, foolish hankering for her father's new registrar, she told herself sensibly—and fled at the first opportunity to the small sitting-room at the end of the corridor that was her bolt-hole in times of crisis.

Only moments later, Verity put her shining blonde head round the door. 'Any objection to company?'

'Of course not.' Stifling an instinctive protest at the intrusion on some very welcome privacy, Jennet hastily thrust her hanky out of sight. She wasn't usually a weepy girl, but all her emotions seemed to be out of control and running away with her, whizzing her up and hurtling her down again like a fairground rollercoaster. 'Coffee . . .?' She reached for another mug.

'Love some.' Verity settled herself into a chair for a heart-to-heart. 'Paul looks well, doesn't he?'

Jennet's heart sank at the introduction of the one subject she was anxious to avoid. She didn't want to talk about Paul and Verity. Not any more. The affair was entirely their business and it was up to them where it led. She had enough to do to master her own troublesome feelings. And, deep down, she was just a little envious of their happiness.

'He seems rested, anyway,' she said in a guarded tone as she spooned granules of instant coffee into the two mugs.

'I'm good for him.' Verity smiled as she realised the complacency of the words. 'That sounds conceited but it's true, you know.'

'I expect you're right.' Setting the mugs on the table, Jennet drew up a chair and sat down with her friend.

Other than hustling Verity from the room and locking the door, or walking out herself, there was no escape, and perhaps talking over someone else's problems would help her to marshal her own thoughts and feelings before she returned to Theatre Three where she must spend the rest of the day in close proximity to the man who had put her heart and mind in such a whirl.

'Paul drank scarcely at all over the weekend,' Verity volunteered. 'I know it wasn't easy for him but he wanted to please me. He *cares* about me, Jennet. It's really important to him that everything should be right for us.'

'Perhaps he sees you as an old man's last chance of happiness,' Jennet said lightly.

Verity bridled, and then laughed as she realised the teasing twinkle in her friend's sparkling eyes. 'That's what it is, of course,' she agreed, with an unshakeable faith in her conviction that it was nothing of the kind.

'But what about you? Seriously, that's what I can't understand, Verity. I can see the *attraction*, of course. Paul's very handsome, very charming, very attractive to women. But you seem to be thinking about him along permanent lines. You ought to fall in and out of love a few times before you even think of settling for one man. Preferably a much younger man,' she added with brutal frankness.

'It isn't just attraction and it *is* permanent,' Verity said firmly.

'Does that mean wedding bells in the near future?' With a smile, Jennet turned the tables on the self-assured young doctor who seemed so sure of a future with Paul.

'Oh, I doubt it. I'm willing to make the commitment, of course. But Paul has this ridiculous conscience about tying me down so young and getting in the way of my career. I'll talk him round, but it may take a little time and I don't see why we shouldn't be together while I'm doing it.' Verity shot a wary glance at her and added, 'I've moved in with him, Jennet. I'm putting my flat on the market.'

Cradling both hands about the untouched mug of coffee, Jennet wondered why she felt neither shock nor surprise at the announcement. She had been so concerned, both for her father and for her friend, but now she felt totally detached from the whole business. If Paul was making a terrible mistake and if Verity was throwing away heart, happiness and career on a man old enough to be her father—well, there was nothing that *she* could do about it.

All she wanted was to be left alone to sort out her own feelings and her own fate . . .

Verity put a tentative hand on the silent theatre sister's arm. 'I'm afraid you mind very much.'

Jennet smiled and squeezed the slim fingers. 'I don't mind at all,' she said with perfect truth. 'I'm only too pleased for Paul if it's really what he wants. And I'm pleased for you, too—truly I am.' On a sudden impulse, she got to her feet and hugged her friend. She could have wished that Paul had broken the news, but she wouldn't cast even a small shadow across Verity's triumph by saying so.

'Then you'll join us in a little celebration this evening? We're inviting just a few friends. Bring Jeff with you, of course. We're both looking forward to meeting him.'

'He's in Liverpool at the moment. On business. But I'll come, certainly . . .' Jennet didn't wish to go but knew that she had no choice. She loved Paul too much to hurt and disappoint him by staying away with the implication of disapproval.

Again she wished that the invitation had come from her father, although she understood the pleasure and satisfaction it gave Verity to use the words 'we' and 'us' in connection with herself and the distinguished consultant who was lover as well as boss.

Jennet devoutly hoped that Verity loved the man and not just the position he held, with all its prestige and social status and the promise of assistance with a clever young doctor's professional career . . .

Whisking through her wardrobe that evening, she finally settled on a cloud of smoke-grey chiffon. Worn only once before, it had been tucked away at the back waiting for the right occasion to be brought out again. This seemed a suitable occasion, Jennet decided. She owed it to Paul to look good, for he loved to show her off to his friends, some of whom had known and still remembered her mother and agreed that Jennet was the image of the lovely girl who had died so tragically young.

Through the years, Paul had kept faith with those old friends, and she wondered how they would react to the introduction of the youthful Verity into their circle. The men would admire her and envy Paul, of course. The middle-aged wives would probably close ranks against the good-looking newcomer until they were satisfied that she posed no threat to their comfortable marriages. While Verity, stunning and self-assured, would capably hold her own in the face of any censure or criticism because she was sure of Paul's loving support and protection.

It must be wonderful to know that kind of confidence, Jennet thought rather wistfully, as she put last-minute touches to her make-up. To love and know oneself truly loved in return was every girl's dream. To put out a hand in the darkest night and know herself safe in the arms of a man who owned her heart and would treasure it for ever was every girl's hope.

But her foolish heart was trying to force itself upon a man who didn't want it, and the best thing she could do was to recapture it as quickly as she could, Jennet told herself sternly, thankful that Duncan couldn't have the slightest suspicion of how she felt about him.

Yet . . .

Dressed and perfumed, her shining hair brushed and swept into a confusion of curls which she had plaited with an orange ribbon that matched the threaded bands through the bodice and skirt of her filmy dress, with a splash of bright orange lipstick complementing the pale translucence of her skin and the clear amber eyes, Jennet studied the reflection of an almost-stranger in the long mirror in her bedroom.

She looked *different*, almost beautiful, she

realised in surprise. The starchy and sometimes straitlaced theatre sister was temporarily submerged in a misty cloud of grey chiffon that gave her an appealing air of fragile femininity.

A slight frown leapt into her eyes as the doorbell pealed. She wasn't expecting anyone, but it might be the unpredictable Jeff, returned early from his business trip and intending to surprise her—and that meant she would have to take him along with her to meet Paul and Verity. Another ten minutes and she would have been on her way . . .

As she opened the door, expecting to see the stocky, medium-height figure of the American, her eyes met the gleaming white shirt-front of a very tall man in a dinner jacket. Her gaze moved swiftly up past the powerful chest and strong column of his throat to the firm jaw, the mobile mouth, the slightly irregular but still handsome nose and then, at last, the amused grey eyes of the last man she had expected to see standing on her doorstep. But wasn't he just as unpredictable as Jeff, in his own way?

'Ready?' Duncan asked lightly.

Just as if she was expecting him! Just as if he hadn't spent much of the day pretending that she didn't exist! Jennet swelled with remembered hurt and fresh indignation. 'I'm not going anywhere with *you!*' she announced flatly.

The surgeon's smile ignored the uncompromising words. 'Paul asked me to pick you up,' he said smoothly. 'I gather your boyfriend has gone out of town.'

He looked down at the pretty girl in her pretty dress with the pretty colour sweeping in and out of her face and no sign of a welcome in her amber eyes and knew he couldn't sustain the angry determination to put her out of heart and mind and life. He loved her.

'Oh . . . there was no need . . .' Jennet found herself floundering before the glow in his eyes and a smile that seemed to wrap her around with its warmth. She struggled with the errant leap of her heart and a kindling urge to strangle her well-meaning father. Why hadn't it occurred to her that Duncan would be a fellow guest that evening? Or, at the very back of her mind, had there been a tiny hope that had influenced her choice of dress, the care she had taken with face and hair, the spray of her most expensive perfume?

'Paul doesn't like the idea of you driving across town and back again later.'

Jennet stiffened at the implication that she needed protecting. 'I'm quite capable——'

'Of looking after yourself. Yes, I know. But it seems unnecessary to use two cars to transport two people, don't you think? It's no trouble to me to take you, Jennet. We *are* going the same way.' Let her be in no doubt that he wouldn't be deflected from loving and wanting and wishing to marry her by a fancy for a transatlantic hero whom she had vested with all kinds of romantic qualities simply because they had met on holiday. Maybe the American *was* a young girl's dream. Duncan knew that *he* was the reality that Jennet needed for her lasting happiness. She would probably call it arrogance if he told her of that conviction. He called it an instinctive awareness of their mutual destiny.

She suppressed a foolish tendency to read more than he meant into the light words, and opened the door wider to admit him. 'I'll just get my wrap . . .'

There was no point in further protest. Paul had decreed and his registrar had agreed. Jennet had no way of knowing how Duncan really felt about the arrangement. He smiled. He seemed friendly, even warm towards her. His manner was relaxed. Was this the man who had snubbed and ignored her for much of the day? The man who had hurt her much more than she would want him to know? Moody, difficult, arrogant and demanding, all the things she most disliked, she thought wryly. Yet he seemed to be the one man who could own her heart and hold her senses in thrall and satisfy all the requirements she had ever thought to look for in a husband.

Tall, powerfully built, Duncan dwarfed the small sitting-room as he surveyed her pictures, her books, her trailing plants and the few but good pieces of porcelain. 'Nice,' he commented. Now, whenever he thought of her—and that was too often for comfort—he would be able to visualise her in these pleasant, lived-in surroundings and feel that much closer to the girl who kept him so determinedly at a distance. 'You live alone, I believe.'

'I do now,' Jennet said from the doorway that connected living-room and bedroom. 'I used to share with a friend. She got married.' She moved into the room, the thin shawl about her shoulders exactly the shade of the ribbons in her dress and hair. Grey, thin-strapped sandals and palest grey silk stockings completed the ensemble.

Duncan's glance swept her with a comprehensive appreciation and she felt a quiver of nervous excitement as she realised the intensity of admiration in his eyes—and something more, something that quickened her pulses, a smoulder that hinted at a fire that might consume them both and for ever if it were once allowed to leap into flame . . .

Their eyes locked for a breathless moment.

In an attempt to break a dangerous spell, Jennet impulsively swirled on high heels, chiffon skirts flaring about her shapely legs, delicate perfume wafting into the room as she spun.

'Very nice,' he said softly, the simple words conveying the depth of his desire for the slender girl with her lovely face and shining cluster of curls and sudden, dazzling smile.

'Thank you.' Jennet dipped a mock curtsy, her eyes dancing. Then, recklessly, she moved closer to him, encouragement in her lingering smile, aware of all the dangers in his desire but spurred by her own fierce hunger for his touch and his kiss.

Duncan's hands were unsteady as they arranged the folds of the shawl that had slipped from her shoulders. His strong fingers grazed her neck and the swell of her breast and she trembled, looking up at him with a widening of beautiful amber eyes, a hint of irresistible invitation in their shining depths.

His breath pent up, he kissed her, his mouth skimming the sweetness from her lips as if taking them more surely would ignite the fierce, invincible flame of a need he was desperately trying to master.

Jennet knew she was hurling herself at him but some strange, compelling insistence drove her on. Wanting him had become an awful pressure of longing in heart and mind and body, a persistent ache in her breast and a bittersweet stir of yearning in most secret places. On a soft, murmuring sigh, she laid her head on the powerful chest with its heavy-beating heart so that Duncan's arms were forced to fold about her . . .

CHAPTER TEN

THE scent and the sweetness of her filled him with desire. She knew what she did, this eternal Eve with her seductive smiles and sighs and soft body pressed close to him, Duncan decided in the brief moment before hesitation was ousted by the sweeping storm of passion. This lovely girl who had moved so eagerly into his arms with a smiling invitation in her amber eyes was no shy virgin, teetering on the edge of a new experience. Here was a woman, his woman, his for the taking . . .

Strong fingers tilted her face and her unsuspecting mouth met the full force of a deep, demanding kiss that shattered her startled senses into a thousand prisms of light and dark and sweet melt of sensation.

Jennet had never been kissed so commandingly or so confidently in all her life, and it left her shaken, breathless and clamouring. The impact of his maleness banished the last vestige of resistance to loving a strong, sensual man who didn't allow anything to stand in the way of what he wanted.

He held her in a fiercely urgent embrace against his rock-hard body with its insistent throb of need, strong hands roving over her back and shoulders and curving about her breasts with an ardour that seemed to burn her sensitive skin through the thin stuff of her dress.

Jennet clung to him, revelling in the taste and the feel and the exciting closeness of him, swept by

a total abandon to her senses and the prompting
of her heart. She gave him kiss for kiss, fingers
delving into the provocative tendrils of chestnut
hair on his neck, straying to tug at shirt buttons
and steal beneath crisp linen to find the warm,
male flesh that quivered at her light, teasing touch.

'Temptress,' he murmured against her lips, tall
frame trembling with the force of his arousal. 'Little
witch . . .'

Jennet felt all the power of a woman to weaken
and humble a man with desire for her and all the
longing of a woman in love to give gladly of herself
for his pleasure and her own. She threw back her
head to look up into darkened grey eyes with the
smoulder of passion in their depths. 'I'm tempted,
too,' she said softly, limpid with love. 'Hold me,
Duncan . . . hold me close . . .'

What man could resist such a plea? Not one who
throbbed so fiercely with love and need. Aflame
with fire she had consciously sparked and fuelled,
how could he reject all that she offered so eagerly?
Duncan suddenly swept her up into his arms and
carried her into the adjoining bedroom.

She was set down gently in the middle of her
bed. Bending over her, he cradled her face in tender
hands and kissed her with such lingering sweetness
that any thought of denying the ecstasy to be found
in his arms promptly died a death.

Jennet held out her arms to him.

Duncan dropped a light kiss on her hair and
straightened. He divested himself of his dinner
jacket and tossed it across a chair. He undid the
careful bow of his black tie and drew it from his
neck to lay on the dressing-table. He unfastened
the buttons of his shirt that her busy fingers had

overlooked.

The spell briefly broken, Jennet leaned up on an elbow. 'What about the party?' she asked uncertainly. 'We're expected . . .'

'To hell with the party,' Duncan said succinctly. He looked at her with a twinkle in his eyes. 'Or perhaps you'd rather . . .?'

She shook her head, a shy smile hovering, a little remorse in her eyes. He knew only too well that she wasn't likely to prefer a dinner party to the promise in his kiss and powerful body.

'Having got this far . . .' She broke off as he sat on the side of the bed, muscles rippling in the strong shoulders and muscular chest that he had bared, and trailed a caressing finger down her cheek and slender throat to the taut swell of her breast.

'I thought we'd never make it,' he said drily. 'The games you women play . . .' He sighed in mock reproach.

Jennet felt an acute dislike of being lumped with all the other women he had known and carelessly loved. It ought to be different! He ought to love her as she loved him! His kiss silenced the instinctive protest of her heart and she was helpless all over again before the charge of love and longing.

Removing a sandal, Duncan caressed the sensitive sole of her foot, the slender ankle and the length of shapely leg and thigh with sweeping strokes of clever hands that knew how to heighten excitement, and then he unfastened the suspender clip and gently rolled the stocking down and off. He repeated the process with the other leg, the sensuality of the small but intimate service sending flickers of flame through her unsuspecting body. Eyes closed and heart pounding and body a confusion of new sensations, Jennet gave herself up to the delicious delight of being undressed and coaxed into surrender by an expert.

It didn't matter that he didn't love her. Perhaps that would come later . . .

'I'd hate to crush that lovely dress,' Duncan murmured, his lips at the warm hollow of her throat and his weight heavy on her breasts.

Jennet hesitated. Then, as he moved away from her, she knelt up on the bed and lifted the dress over her head. It fell in a froth of chiffon to the floor. Suddenly self-conscious before the warm study of his eyes, she crossed her arms over the lacy bra that only just covered the swell of her breasts.

Duncan kissed her bare shoulder. 'You're gorgeous,' he said softly. 'The loveliest girl in the world. Jennet, I want you so much.'

Her body tingled as he unclipped the scrap of lace with hands that shook, and tossed it to join her dress on the floor. Tenderly cradling the small, beautiful breasts, he paid lover's homage to each in turn, lips trailing over warm, sweet flesh to the quivering, expectant tip. Jennet trembled from head to toe as fierce darts of desire pierced her with each sure sweep of caressing lips and tongue.

On a sudden shaft of longing, she put both hands to his dark chestnut head and tried to draw him down to her. She ached for the pleasure of flesh on flesh, hard thrust of maleness initiating her into the delights of a world she had never known.

Duncan resisted. '*Wait*, my lovely . . .'

Jennet didn't think that she *could*. She was consumed with the need to know the delicious secret of loving between a man and a woman. But she was too shy to insist and too inexperienced to know how to compel him with kiss and intimate caress to take her with him to the ultimate ecstasy on a tidal flood of passion.

He continued to make slow and very sensual love to her with lips and exploring hands until she was a bright flame of ungovernable fire. She almost stormed at him for taking her high, high, high only to bring her hurtling down again, time after time, but she forgave him on a breathless sigh of anticipation as he finally stretched his lean body, naked and aware, alongside her and submitted to her caresses.

Duncan was thankful for the mastery of desire that came with experience and understanding of a woman's needs. He wanted this first time with Jennet to be without haste and forever remembered. But the seemingly shy touch and the sweetness of her offered lips and the welcome of soft breasts and thighs were too much for any man's resolution. And he loved her.

With a groan, he swept her suddenly beneath him as love and need and longing broke all bounds.

As his lips came down to claim her and his proud, powerful body took her virginity at a passionate stroke, Jennet drowned in dark, delicious delight and clung, melting and molten with love, as every sense and tingling nerve and quivering fibre gloried in the soaring pleasure of his embrace.

Her tumbled curls fell about her face and neck and Duncan twined his fingers through them and whispered her name again and again through tumultuous kisses as their joyous bodies mounted the highest peak and tumbled together down the other side on a rush of ecstatic fulfilment.

Passion spent, but love burning fierce in him,

Duncan held her close to his heart, his face buried in the perfume of her glorious hair.

Jennet felt the heavy thud of his heart and tasted the salt of his sweat on his bare shoulder as she kissed the warm, moist flesh. He lifted his head to smile at her and she saw a deep contentment in the grey eyes that she searched with a little anxiety. Like every woman, she needed to know that she had no rival in the art of love. She wanted to be assured that he had found supreme satisfaction in her arms so that he would never want any other woman for as long as he lived.

'Was it good?' she asked shyly.

'*Good*!' Duncan laughed aloud, sheer male triumph in the sound. 'God, you are incredible, Jennet! Don't you know that it was splendid, superb, the most fantastic experience of my life? There's never been anyone like you. You're special—a very special woman.' He kissed her, quick and hard, warm with delight at the unexpected innocence in her anxious, amber eyes.

He had known at the moment of most intimate contact that the virginal quality that had drawn him to love her was no deception. He felt proud and humbled and very happy to have been the recipient of her most precious gift. If nothing else, if she never loved him, at least she would never, ever forget him, he thought on a surge of satisfaction.

'I'm glad,' Jennet said simply, nestling into arms that closed so surely about her that she felt she would be safe in them for the rest of her life. She was glad that she loved him. She was glad that he had been the first to take her to that heaven on earth where man and woman met and loved and gloried in a mutual and very powerful passion.

Duncan brushed her lips in an infinitely tender kiss, ready to commit himself completely to a woman for the first time in his life. 'You're special because I love you,' he said softly.

The quiet words and the thump of her heart were drowned by the sudden clamour of the telephone at the side of the bed. Jennet couldn't be sure that she'd heard alright or if he meant what might just be the impulsive declaration of a sexually satisfied man. Love to someone like Duncan might be a very different emotion from the force that had swept and seized and altered her life, after all.

Duncan growled an obscenity. 'Ignore it,' he commanded. He ran a sensual hand over her slender back, delighting in the shudder that instantly rippled through her still-sensitive body.

Jennet tried, burying her face in the strong male scent of his muscular chest. But the shrill insistence of sound dispelled the magic and she couldn't lose herself in the wonderful world of love that beckoned. The part of her that adored the man who held her so warmly fought the intrusion of the outside world, but the trained nurse instinctively answered the summons of the telephone.

'I can't——!' she wailed, and wriggled from under him to reach a hand to lift the receiver.

'Jennet . . .? It's me—Verity! I felt I ought to warn you that Paul's asked Duncan Blair to call for you. Knowing how you feel about the man . . .'

'It's all right, Verity. He's here.' Jennet wondered if the quiver in her voice as Duncan kissed the sensitive spot at the base of her spine told her friend that she had telephoned at an inopportune moment. It could have been worse. Verity could have dialled the number a few minutes earlier and saved her from a fate supposedly worse than death but which was, in fact, rather like hurtling over the threshold into paradise at the splintering moment of climax.

'Oh! Then you didn't shut the door in his face?' Verity teased.

'Not quite.' Warm colour swept into her face as Duncan's roaming hands found and cupped her breasts and he mischievously pressed himself against her naked back and nuzzled the nape of her neck with his lips. Thankful that visiphones had not yet become a commonplace in every home, Jennet dug him with an elbow that caught him in such a vulnerable spot that he grunted in surprise. Hastily, she covered the mouthpiece and turned to frown at him. 'Yes, I do know that Paul wants us to be friends. I don't think it's at all likely,' she said firmly into the telephone.

'Why not?' Duncan demanded in mock indignation, almost loud enough for Verity to catch the words.

'Much too late,' she murmured drily. Then, to Verity, 'I said of course we won't be late. In fact, we're on the point of leaving.'

'Like that?' Duncan's eyebrows soared almost to disappearing point beneath the thatch of his thick wavy hair.

Jennet giggled. 'Sssh . . .!'

'Not that *I've* any objection, of course.' He appraised her splendid nudity with satisfaction and chuckled at her sweet confusion.

'What *is* going on there?' Verity demanded in sudden, amused suspicion.

'Nothing at all,' Jennet assured her airily, crossing her fingers as she uttered the lie, and

Duncan shook his head in mock reproach, laughter brimming in grey eyes.

'No, I guess not. You aren't the type.' Verity's dry words sounded almost like disapproval of the old-fashioned principles that had kept Jennet a virgin until she had fallen headlong into love.

'Little does *she* know,' Duncan said complacently as Jennet hastily rang off. Verity's clear tones had carried sufficiently for him to hear almost every word of the brief exchange.

Jennet stiffened. 'I'm *not* the type. Not in the way that Verity means—or *you* might think,' she said hotly. Their lovemaking had been so right, so natural in the way it had come about that she didn't want it smirched and cheapened in any way.

'Whatever I thought, you've proved me wrong, haven't you?' His voice was gentle. So was the touch of his lips on her breast, a lover's reverent kiss. Involuntarily, she laid a hand on the thick, crisp waves of his chestnut hair, filling with love for him. 'Sweet Jennet, lovely Jennet, I'm glad I got to first base before your American friend. I bet it isn't for want of trying, damn him!'

'Jealous?' Suddenly, she was all woman, head tilted, a provocative smile in the amber eyes as she teased him.

'I'll hurl him through the nearest window if I ever catch him making love to my woman,' Duncan said savagely, meaning it. He caught her close. 'You *are* my woman, Jennet. This is where you belong. In *my* arms.'

Until he tired of her or found someone else, she thought, anxiety clutching at her heart. You were fantastic, you're special, he had said in the euphoria of after-loving. She might be sexually inexperienced but she wasn't a fool, and she knew it would be dangerous to believe that his words implied a commitment or a lasting passion. There's never been anyone like you, he had claimed—but loving was always twinned with the fear of losing and there was a tight knot of apprehension in Jennet's breast. A man who had got what he wanted so easily might not value it, and she had given him so much more than her precious virginity. She had given him her heart.

'We *are* going to be late—dreadfully late!' she abruptly exclaimed, conscious of smudged make-up and tousled hair and knowing that she must shower and dress and make herself presentable before they could set off for Paul's apartment.

'I don't want to go.' Duncan nuzzled her neck. 'Can't we stay here and make love? Ring Paul, make some excuse . . .'

'I don't want to go, either.' She sighed. 'But we must!' She thrust him away with determined hands before his nearness and dearness could undermine her resistance.

As the powerful Jaguar nosed through the steady stream of traffic heading for the riverside, Duncan took a hand from the steering wheel to cover the slim fingers that were so tightly locked in Jennet's lap. 'Regrets?' She was so still, so silent, that he was anxious. A woman could undergo a sudden revulsion of feeling towards the man who had shared her first experience of sexual delight, and he didn't have the confidence of knowing that Jennet cared enough for him to overcome it. She might not want to have anything more to do with him after that evening, he thought wryly, recalling the time it had taken to break down her defensive hostility and apparent dislike.

Jennet shook her head, smiled. She was quiet because she was remembering, reliving magic moments, revelling in their new-found intimacy and understanding. Doubts and fears were thrust to the back of her mind for the time being and she delighted in being with the man she loved. Handsome, clever, caring and proven to be the perfect lover, she thought happily—and did it matter how and when he had gained his expertise? She closed her mind to the thought of the women in his past and determined to be the only woman in his future. Positive thinking could work wonders, she told herself firmly.

'What on earth happened to you?' Verity, elegant and looking older in sophisticated black satin, drew them eagerly into the apartment. 'Paul has been quite anxious . . .'

'Nonsense! Paul knew you were in good hands,' he amended smoothly with a light slap of Duncan's broad shoulder and a smile for Jennet.

'Sorry . . .' Jennet met her father's searching, slightly quizzical gaze with the hint of a blush. 'The traffic was so heavy,' she said lamely.

'It's quite a trek across town,' Paul agreed. The colour in her face and the sparkle in her eyes made him suspect that the couple had been quarrelling during the journey. Usually Jennet got on so well with everyone, but it seemed that sparks flew whenever she came into contact with Blair. A case of 'I do not love you, Dr Fell', no doubt. He put an arm about her. 'Come and say hello to Helen and George . . .' As they crossed the room together, he lowered his voice. 'Sorry about that, sweetheart. Thrusting you into Blair's company, I mean. Verity tells me that you don't like him overmuch.'

Jennet looked up quickly, wondering what her father would say if she told him just how much she liked his new registrar and exactly what had happened between them that evening. Couldn't he tell just by looking at her? Wasn't it written all over her for the whole world to see? She could only marvel that such a mystical, magical and utterly memorable experience should have left no obvious mark!

Embraced by her father's friends and her conversation monopolised, Jennet looked across the room to Duncan. Verity had brought him a drink and stayed to talk, leaning against him in laughing intimacy. Jennet's heart lurched jealously as she realised their closeness, their affection for each other.

Sick dismay welled as she wondered if she had been *used*. Had Duncan deliberately kissed and fondled her while she talked to Verity on the telephone because he hoped that their new-found intimacy would be conveyed along the wire and give her friend something to think about? Was he hoping to lure Verity from Paul's arms by bringing home to her what she was missing when she spurned a younger man with so much more to offer?

Had he only taken her because he couldn't have Verity and he needed to assuage the ache for her in any woman's arms? Seeing the warmth in his grey eyes and the tenderness in his smile and the meaningful pressure of Verity's hand as it rested on his arm, Jennet felt that it must be so.

And she had been near to believing the soft-spoken words that had been blurred by the ring of the telephone . . .

CHAPTER ELEVEN

WHAT now? Did Duncan's taking of her as if by
royal right mean that they would continue to be
lovers, if only for a time? Or had he already lost
interest and resumed the pursuit of Verity, who was
more encouraging than she ought to be in the
circumstances?

Whatever happened, she would hang on to her
pride even if she had thrown her heart away on a
man who didn't want it. There was no need for
Duncan to know that she loved him, Jennet told
herself proudly, as she looked at the man who
seemed to have forgotten all about her as he talked
to her friend. Then, catching her glance, he smiled
and her foolish heart soared and shivers of
remembered delight rippled down her spine.

An impulsive, answering smile lit up her lovely
face with such brilliance that Paul's dark eyes
narrowed in sudden, pleased suspicion as he
observed the recipient of that golden smile. If that
proved to be a match, he would be delighted—and
a little relieved on his own account, too. Any man
in his position would feel threatened by a younger
man, and he too had noticed that his registrar and
Verity got on very well together.

Throughout the evening, Jennet's mood swung
between elation and dread. Elation whenever
Duncan singled her out with a word or a smile that
seemed secret and special and filled her with
quivering hope. Dread that she had fallen deeply

141

in love with a heartless charmer when she saw him smile and speak to Verity in a way that seemed just as secret and special to her jealous eyes.

A mass of mixed-up emotions, she ignored Duncan for much of the evening, avoiding his querying gaze and refusing to risk even the seemingly accidental brush of hands. Then, woman-like, she fretted and fumed when he followed her lead. She didn't expect to have all his attention that evening, of course. That would be unreasonable, she told herself firmly—and then, with all the unreasoning jealousy of a woman in love, resented every word, every smile, every glance that wasn't directed at herself.

After dinner the party snowballed, for both Paul and Verity had invited friends to join them in celebrating the public announcement of their love for each other. Their engagement came as a shock to Jennet, although she had come to realise that Verity was a very determined girl, and she didn't doubt that she would have her way about marriage in the very near future, in spite of Paul's doubts and demurs.

She glanced instinctively at Duncan but his handsome face was giving nothing away. It was impossible to know what he felt about that declared intention to marry, but he wasn't the kind of man to admit defeat, Jennet felt. Not even when the woman he wanted wore another man's ring—and that enormous sapphire on Verity's left hand wasn't easily overlooked!

She reached to kiss her tall, handsome father as he paused before her with some anxiety in his dark eyes. 'Congratulations!' It was dutiful rather than glad, she realised too late.

'Be happy for me, Jennet,' Paul said quietly. 'I love her very much.' It was a plea for understanding as well as her blessing.

'Be happy for yourself,' Jennet told him with a quick, warm smile. 'She loves you, too.' How could she doubt it as she looked at the girl on Paul's arm, brimming with happiness? Maybe it wouldn't last. Maybe Verity would fall out of love just as surely as she had fallen into it. In the meantime, she had lifted a brilliant surgeon out of a dangerous depression and given him a reason not to drink as well as a new vitality and a new upsurge of enthusiasm for his work. Loving and admiring her father as she did, Jennet had to be grateful to her friend for that, at least. She turned to Verity. 'Just don't expect me to call you Mother!' she teased, the light words camouflaging a full heart.

'I'll hate you if you do!' Verity hugged her affectionately, thankful that Jennet had taken the surprise engagement so well. 'Now you know why we were so anxious when you were late! There was no way that we'd announce our engagement unless you were here and the party would have fallen rather flat. A celebration without an event!'

'I said there was nothing to worry about, darling,' Paul interposed. 'I knew we could rely on Duncan to bring Jennet.'

Good old reliable Duncan nearly let you down, Jennet retorted silently, as the couple moved on to receive more congratulations and good wishes from friends and colleagues.

It seemed that Duncan had known what was in the wind that evening. Perhaps that was one more reason why he had made love to her and tried to persuade her to forgo the party, knowing her presence was felt by Paul and Verity to be essential to the announcement of their engagement, and hoping to delay the inevitable by any means in his power.

Every reason but the right and only one, she thought heavily . . .

Someone put a glass of wine into her hand. She looked up into warm grey eyes. 'Oh . . . thank you . . .' She didn't want the wine. She was warmed by the concern that had brought him to her side. Her heart rocked as she met the impact of a smile that had swept her into loving and giving and heaven here on earth.

'You look shell-shocked,' Duncan said gently.

'Do I?' She smiled. 'Things are happening too fast for me, I'm afraid.' She would never forget all that had happened this night if she lived to be a thousand years old, she thought wryly.

Duncan led her out to the roof-garden with its greenery and shaded lights and comfortable rattan furniture. She had been warding him off all evening and he had understood that she needed time to reflect, to consider how she felt about him, to decide if they had a future. Now, he felt that she needed him. Loving her father, doing her best to see him through a bad patch, she was hurt that all her efforts had paled before the bright illumination of a love that had completely changed Paul's life.

'You must have seen it coming,' he suggested.

'Not *marriage*—no!' Jennet sank on to a cushioned two-seater sofa, struggling with a shaming envy. Lucky Verity to be so loved . . .

'They *aren't* married. Not yet.'

'Do you think it won't happen? They're lovers. They're living together. Marriage is the next step, surely?'

'It should be. But it doesn't always happen that way, does it? And Verity can do better for herself.'

'You said that before! Do you have a particular man in mind?' Jennet wondered if he would admit that it was himself. Could he be that casual so soon after making love to *her*?

Duncan shrugged. 'Ben Drummond. Tim Gowan. John Bentley. Any man of her own age or thereabouts,' he said indifferently.

'She wants Paul.'

'I have to agree with you,' he conceded drily. 'She's made it very plain that she wants Paul. He didn't stand a chance in the face of so much determination.'

Jennet looked up at him. 'Is that all it takes?'

'It depends on what you want and how much you want it, I guess.' His sudden smile was warm, tenderly intimate. 'I wanted you from the first moment I saw you and I didn't let anything stand in *my* way, Jennet. Not even my American rival.'

'Don't gloat!' she said sharply. 'It could just as easily have been Jeff. The mood and the moment combined, that's all.' There had been more to it than that but, far from sure where she stood in this man's reckoning, she wasn't going to tell him that it had happened because she loved him and he was the only man for her.

'And the man wasn't important. Is that what you're saying?' Duncan challenged harshly. He had lit a candle to her loveliness and dearness with his lovemaking and its flame would burn for ever in his memory, whatever happened. He knew better than to take anything for granted. Especially a woman. But it hurt and angered him that Jennet could speak so dismissively of that shared, enriching experience.

'No . . . I . . . not exactly . . .' A flurry of agitation among the assembled guests in the room behind them and a loud wail of protest silenced the floundering words. In an instant, Jennet was on her feet, a clutch at her heart telling her that something had happened to her father.

People clustered about Paul's unconscious form as he lay on the floor, grey-faced and slack-mouthed and looking suddenly much older than his years. Jennet thrust her way into the centre of the group and dropped to her knees beside her father.

'He's arrested,' someone told her unnecessarily. 'He was talking to me one moment and the next . . .'

'He isn't——?' She broke off, relief flooding. Paul's breathing was shallow and stertorous but he *was* breathing.

'Oh, God! Oh, no! Oh, someone help him do something! *Please!*' Verity sobbed piteously as she stroked Paul's face and dark head with shaking hands, cradling him in her lap. The self-possessed young doctor had gone completely to pieces in the face of an emergency that affected the man she loved.

There were more than enough medical men in the room but Duncan took charge by tacit consent. As Paul's second-in-command and a specialist in cardiac malfunction, he was well equipped to handle the situation.

'Get Paul's bag, Jennet,' he commanded forcefully as he knelt on the floor at her side. 'There will be drugs in it that we can use . . . hurry! Verity, pull yourself together and get out of the way. You aren't helping. Everyone else, please stand back. Has anyone called an ambulance?'

Someone had. 'It's on its way.'

Jennet scrambled to her feet and ran to Paul's study for his medical bag and then began a frantic search for keys. They were eventually discovered on a chain that hung from his belt. By then, Duncan had begun artificial respiration. Paul was in total collapse, no sign of pulse or respiration, pupils dilated, no longer breathing.

Verity was still sobbing, being soothed and comforted by a guest who was trying to persuade her from the room.

Jennet had no time to feel sorry for her shattered friend as she unlocked Paul's bag and found the required drugs as well as a number of sealed hypodermic syringes.

She felt detached, totally divorced from the proceedings, as her practised hands broke open the ampoules and filled the syringes . . . adrenaline to stimulate the action of the heart, sodium bicarbonate to correct acidosis, lignocaine to restore the regular rhythm of contractions once the heart began to beat again. Ben Drummond took over the work of artificial respiration as Duncan took each filled syringe in turn from Jennet's surprisingly steady hand and injected the life-saving drugs into Paul's heart and veins.

When the ambulance arrived a few minutes later, Paul was still unconscious but breathing again and his heart, though sluggish, was pumping the vital blood along his veins to the brain. There was every chance that prompt action had prevented serious damage.

Shortly afterwards, he was installed in the Intensive Care Unit of a nearby hospital, wired up to monitors and surrounded by drips, seriously ill but alive.

'As soon as he's stable he can be transferred to the Fitz,' Duncan promised the distraught Verity. 'But he's in very good hands here, you know.'

The London Collegiate was the hospital where he had worked for some years before Paul had persuaded him to join the Cardiac Unit at the Fitz as his senior registrar. Familiar with its work as well as with many of its staff, he could be reassuring.

'How *could* it happen to him?' Verity asked helplessly. 'He was fine! There was no indication . . . he was well, happy, relaxed . . .'

'Stress,' Duncan said tersely. 'Frida's death, drinking heavily, anxiety about his job and about you, too, Verity. He felt that he was taking advantage of you and denying you the chance to find happiness with a younger man. It's preyed on his mind more than you realise, I think. Tonight . . . well, happiness can be a killer, too. A sudden surge of adrenalin . . .' He lifted his broad shoulders in a shrug. He turned to Jennet. 'Take her home and see that she gets some sleep. Try to rest yourself. There's nothing that either of you can do here for the time being.'

'She won't go. Nor will I. Not until we're sure that Paul's going to be all right,' Jennet returned with the obstinate streak she had inherited from her father.

Duncan understood. Briefly, he put a comforting hand on her shoulder. 'I'll be around . . .'

She nodded, too numb with shock and anxiety

to react to his touch, the warmth of eyes and voice. 'Thank you.' The quiet words couldn't convey how she felt. Her gratitude, her deep thankfulness, her relief. He had certainly saved Paul's life that evening. No matter that there had been half a dozen others at the party who could have done exactly the same. It was Duncan who had moved swiftly and surely into action and brought Paul back from the brink of death.

Duncan. And Paul, her father. The two men that she loved. Jennet didn't think she could bear to lose either of them . . .

The two girls kept vigil through a night during which Paul suffered another two attacks, less severe than the first but harmful to an already damaged heart. They waited and prayed, drinking interminable cups of coffee, asking each other questions to which they already knew the answers. No one could be sure that Paul would live. No one could say how badly affected in mind and body he might be if he recovered.

Duncan reported to them at regular intervals after liaising with the unit staff. His calm, his confidence, soothed them both. His presence at the hospital was a comfort to Jennet although she recognised that his main concern was for Verity, quieter now, coming to terms, but obviously blaming herself to some extent. Again and again, she echoed Duncan's warning that happiness could also kill until Jennet wished devoutly that he had never uttered the unthinking words.

It was a long night but, as morning brought the first of the daily routines that marked the hospital day, Paul was said to be in a stable condition and both girls were allowed a brief glimpse of him as he lay in the side ward, grey and still, the bleep of the attached monitor assuring them that his heartbeat had steadied.

Duncan caught Verity as she slumped, overcome with a mix of relief and guilt. Lifting her easily, he placed her on a convenient trolley out in the corridor and sent a nurse for brandy.

'She's taken it badly,' he said, chafing Verity's cold hands while Jennet discreetly adjusted the skirt that exposed her friend's slender thigh. 'She's very shocked. She's been uptight for weeks about her job and this business with your father.' He shot a glance at Jennet, frowning at the smudge of shadow beneath her lovely eyes and the pallor of her cheeks. 'Are *you* all right?'

'I'm fine.' A faint smile flickered.

He nodded approval. 'Good. You're strong. Tougher than you look, aren't you? Verity's not as fit as she could be right now. Overworked, rushed meals, not enough sleep—and now this. She needs some time off. I'll see that she gets it.'

Jennet felt his words and manner like a physical stab to the heart. Perhaps she *was* tough, cool-headed in a crisis, but at that moment she envied the fragile, helpless Verity, fussed over and cosseted by a man who cared more than anyone, perhaps even he, had realised. The look on his handsome face as he'd caught the fainting girl, the concern in his eyes and voice, the tenderness of much more than ordinary affection in the way he warmed Verity's hands in his own as he watched and waited for her to come round, told its own story to her vulnerable mind.

Eyelids fluttered. Verity struggled to sit up and then burst into tears. The nurse arrived with the brandy. Jennet supported her friend while Duncan held the glass to Verity's trembling lips.

She drank a little, choked and spluttered, drank again and then took a deep, sighing breath as the colour began to return to her cheeks. 'I feel such a fool . . .' She put her face into Duncan's powerful chest like a child seeking comfort.

He patted her shoulder, stroked the pale wing of blonde hair from her face. 'What's a faint between friends?' he soothed, smiling into the troubled eyes. 'You're OK. Things just got on top of you, that's all. I'm going to take you home right now . . .'

'You can stay with me, Verity. You won't want to be on your own at the moment,' Jennet volunteered quickly.

Verity was her friend, no matter what. Eventually, when Paul was well again, she would become her stepmother. In the meantime, Paul would want her to take care of Verity. No one could expect her to return to the apartment with its chaos of half-finished drinks and overflowing ashtrays and rumpled cushions, the general disorder of a party abruptly abandoned on the collapse of the host. There was really no reason why Verity shouldn't stay with her until she felt like going back to her own flat, which had not yet been put into the hands of estate agents.

Even in her own thoughts, Jennet wouldn't put into words the possibility that neither Paul nor Verity would return to live in the luxurious apartment that overlooked the River Thames . . .

Duncan dropped both girls at the door of Pilgrim House on his way to the Fitz to step into Paul's shoes. Temporarily, he stressed. It might be some time before Paul was well enough to resume work. In the meantime, he would take over the responsibility for his clinics and rounds and operating lists. As he had done on too many occasions in the short time that he had been Paul's senior registrar. There had been murmurs about the consultant's neglect of his duties but they would be silenced now by his illness. No doubt it would be assumed that an impending heart attack had been the cause rather than the result of his recent eccentric behaviour. Duncan intended to further that belief.

'Take care of her,' he said to Jennet with an anxious jerk of his head at Verity, standing on the pavement with a lost and bewildered expression.

'Of course I will . . .' Jennet understood his concern for her friend. It hurt that he seemed to overlook *her* shock, *her* anxiety about Paul, the emotional upheaval of *her* traumatic night. All his thought was for Verity. She disliked herself for being jealous of her friend at such a time but she couldn't help the flow of bitter feeling.

Duncan covered the hand that rested on the edge of the open window of his impatiently thrumming Jaguar as it stood at the kerbside. 'I'll be in touch.' The deepening of his voice and the pressure of his fingers did their best to convey all that he felt but thought tactless to speak in front of the listening Verity. Jennet would understand. She knew that he loved her. She must also be sure in her heart that he hoped she would learn to love him and agree to marry him one day.

He drove away as the two girls turned towards the entrance, Jennet's comforting arm about her friend. She would have her hands full with Verity, he thought wryly. The young doctor's surprising lack of control betrayed that she had little experience of personal grief. Whereas Jennet had never known her mother, and her father had been a virtual stranger until she began her training at the hospital where he held a consultancy. Only that year, she had lost her stepmother in tragic circumstances. The years of nursing at the Fitz had taught her to cope with all kinds of emotional upsets, while an innate sweetness of nature had kept her from becoming hardened. Jennet's warmth of heart, her sensitivity and her tender vulnerability were only some of the qualities that had drawn Duncan to love her.

Jennet opened her bedroom door to a rush of memories. It seemed an eternity since she had lain in Duncan's arms in this very room although it was only a matter of twelve hours or so. Would she have let him make love to her if she had known that he cared so much for Verity? The rush of blood in her veins and the weakness of her flesh and the impetus of loving and wanting such as she had never known before might have made it impossible for her to deny him—or herself.

She didn't know what the future held—and here she skated swiftly away from the awful possibility that Paul would die, and Duncan would be on hand to comfort his grieving fiancée and perhaps pave the way to his own happiness at the same time—but she knew with all her heart that she would love Duncan for the rest of her life . . .

CHAPTER TWELVE

EACH day that Paul got through without another and possibly fatal heart attack was a bonus, Jennet felt. Her last thought at night was a prayer for her father and her first act every morning was to telephone the hospital for news.

Perhaps because she was a sister at the Fitz or because Duncan had thoughtfully paved the way with his former colleague at the London Collegiate, the cardiologist in charge was more forthcoming than he might have been. He held out very little hope for Paul, but that was one item of information that Jennet did not pass on to her anxious friend, who had accepted the invitation to stay but was seldom at the flat except to sleep.

Almost frantic with worry, quite incapable of carrying out any of her duties as a doctor, Verity spent most of her time with Paul, although he was so heavily sedated that it was impossible to know if he was aware of her presence at his bedside.

Any doubt that Jennet had felt as to the strength and extent of Verity's feeling for Paul was completely banished. So was any doubt about Duncan's devotion to Verity. He was very supportive, telephoning, calling at the flat to comfort and reassure the distressed young doctor, driving her to and from the hospital when he was free to do so, taking her out for meals to ensure that she ate something and apparently always on call to Verity although he was very busy that week

154

with Paul's work and his own.

Jennet did her best to stifle jealousy and camouflage hurt. There was no hint in Duncan's attitude of the lover that he had briefly been, and he made no attempt to have a private word or moment with her. He treated her like a friend whom he had known for years. That was warming, in a way. But disappointing. She didn't want to be merely a friend to the man she loved.

She wanted him to hold her close and assure her that there was nothing to worry about and that Paul would soon be well enough to dance at *their* wedding as well as his own. She ached for him to kiss her and tell her that he loved her and couldn't be happy without her. She yearned to be sure that she really was special to him, so special that he wouldn't rest until she agreed to marry him. But there was no hint of anything like that in eyes or voice or smile during those first difficult days when she was so anxious about Paul.

She wondered if he was merely holding back until Paul was better and she could be expected to be in a more receptive frame of mind, or if the hour that they had spent in such intimate embrace had meant so little to him that it was already forgotten. Whichever, it might never have happened . . .

Prompted by a mix of pain and pride, she warmly welcomed Jeff's return to London and proceeded to lean on him as if to show Duncan that she didn't need *his* sympathy and support. Maybe it was foolish bravado. But she obeyed the instincts of a jealous heart and ignored the caution of her usually level head that she could alienate a man who was too proud to compete with a rival.

Aware that the Fitz suffered from a chronic

shortage of theatre sisters, she was soon back at work, thankful to have something to occupy her mind as well as the hands that longed to reach out to Duncan but could at least be useful to him as she worked beside him in Theatre Three. Those experienced hands swabbed, passed a variety of instruments, prepared syringes and dressed wounds while taking care not to betray by so much as a tremor that her heart shook at the registrar's nearness.

It was hot beneath the arc lights. Duncan turned his capped head towards her in mute request and Jennet took a towel and wiped the trickle of sweat from his brow, routine service carried out on a sudden rush of a love that had come unbidden and at first unwelcome to find a permanent place in her heart and her life.

Having reached a difficult part of the procedure that required all his concentration, Duncan turned back to the patient without even a cursory nod of thanks. Jennet knew that he was preoccupied rather than indifferent, so there was no rhyme or reason to the flood of hurt except that his brusqueness seemed to be one more brick in the wall that was growing up between them, cemented by her conviction that he was very much in love with Verity.

She could forgive him for taking her as a substitute in a moment of disappointment and despair and anger, having learnt that he had lost all hope of winning Verity. She could even swallow the bitter gall of being second-best. But it would never happen again, she determined.

It was vital to Jennet that Duncan should never know how she felt about him and be sorry that he had swept her into loving when he had only meant to sweep her into bed. She might have lost her heart and her virginity to her father's new registrar but she still had her pride.

There seemed to be no point in loving, in giving, in hoping and dreaming, she thought bleakly. No doubt she would be better off forgetting all about Duncan Blair—and that might entail giving up her job and putting as many miles between them as possible.

But not yet. Not while Paul was so ill . . .

Duncan straightened, flexing hands that ached slightly from the long session of cutting, clamping, probing and ligating. He studied Jennet as she threaded a length of suture silk, her beautiful eyes concentrated on the task, her slim hands admirably sure and steady. As usual, she was the crisply efficient theatre sister who wouldn't allow personal feelings to intrude on her work and, as a dedicated surgeon who could immerse himself in a difficult procedure in spite of an inner turmoil, Duncan approved the detachment of a highly trained nurse.

But it troubled him that Jennet was just as detached and even distant when they were both off duty. She had put up barriers that kept him at bay. That glorious hour of loving might never have been and he was at a loss for the first time in his life where a woman was concerned.

Loving was the very devil! It made a man wary of saying or doing the wrong thing and made him ultra-sensitive to the slightest suggestion of a rebuff. He simply didn't know where he stood with Jennet—and it was scarcely the time to pursue the matter when she was so anxious about her father and so heavily involved with Verity's distress.

Jennet wasn't trying to avoid him. It was scarcely possible for her to do so, in the circumstances, he thought drily. And perhaps she was merely being as discreet as hospital etiquette demanded when she behaved so formally in Theatres. But she was exactly the same when they ran into each other outside the operating theatre. She restricted conversation to the discussion of patients and procedures or Paul's condition or Verity's frame of mind, and escaped as soon as she could with the perfectly valid excuse that she was going to visit her father or had to get home to cook a meal for Verity or was meeting a friend.

Duncan didn't doubt that the friend in question was the American, back in London and apparently as much of a fixture in Jennet's life as before. It was only a step from suspicion to the jealous conviction that the man meant more to Jennet than he ever could and that she was keeping him at a distance because she was anxious not to be reminded, or for the American to learn, of that momentary lapse of loyalty.

'It could just as easily have been Jeff . . .' The words that Jennet had tossed at him that night were a burning brand on his memory. Had it really been just a matter of stirred emotions and lost control on Jennet's part, the fact that he was *there*, holding her, kissing her, compelling her with the urgency of his need, while the man she really cared about was temporarily out of reach?

Had she succumbed to him only because a dormant sexuality had been awakened by another man and the storm of his passionate persuasion had completed an arousal that was strong enough to sweep her off her feet? Had he rushed her into a lovemaking that she now regretted and meant to give him no opportunity to repeat?

And—the one thought that gave him bad nights and provided even more of a spur to a normally quick temper—had that swift, sweet consummation not only left Jennet unconvinced that they had been destined for each other but also crystallised a vague stir of love for another man into a certainty?

It seemed that way . . .

'Almost done, Sister.' Duncan took the threaded needle-holder from her hand with a reassuring smile in his grey eyes. It had been a long day and she must be tired, he thought with tender concern. He was tired, too, but he would work on for some time with another theatre sister to assist him. He was putting in very long days, partly because he was doing the work of two men that week and partly because it left him less time to think and fret about Jennet's attitude and its probable implications. He might be deeply in love but he could still manage to be single-minded during surgery.

'You've been very quick with this one.' Jennet's quiet tone disguised admiration for a superb performance.

'You've cut about ten minutes off the Guv'nor's record,' Tim Gowan put in admiringly. 'Speed as well as proficiency—the hallmark of a good surgeon.'

'Take care what you're doing with that retractor!' Duncan admonished sharply, impatient with praise even when he knew it to be well earned. He had spent fifteen years perfecting his craft and he didn't need to be told by a junior colleague that he was good at his job. A surgeon who didn't know exactly what he was doing in the theatre had no right to take on the life-or-death responsibility for his patients.

While he sutured with deft hands, Jennet busily counted swabs, checked the number of used instruments and opened a sterile pack of dressings, routine tasks that kept her from making too much of a glancing smile and the hint of warm concern in Duncan's deep voice.

She reminded her foolish heart that he was a charmer. Making light love to women with eyes and voice and smile was probably second nature to him and it didn't mean anything when his gaze caught and held her own and the glow of his smile lightened the weight on her breast, or when the brief pressure of his hand filled her with memories of a shared and glorious intimacy. She was just one more woman who had briefly known the kiss, the touch and the ardent embrace of a sensual surgeon.

How could she trust what she thought she saw in those compelling grey eyes, what she thought she had heard him say to her in a moment of exultant triumph? She had hesitated to do so at the time. Now, she told herself firmly that she was just clutching at straws.

Surely, if Duncan felt even a fraction of love for her, he couldn't be so cool, so casual, so caught up in work that was almost routine to a surgeon of his experience that he had no time to assure her with a kiss, a whisper of endearment, that he still thought of her as someone special?

Not here and not now, of course. Even in Jennet's most wistful dreams, Duncan didn't crush her to that powerful, green-garbed chest and kiss her passionately in the middle of complex surgery with the hiss of respirator and the bleep of monitor and the shocked gasps of theatre staff as an accompaniment to his declaration of lasting love.

He was a surgeon, first and foremost. If, by some miracle, he ever came to love her as she loved him, such moments would still be reserved for when they were both off duty, she knew. And, to a theatre sister whose life had revolved around constant concern and loving care for patients since her first days at the Fitz, that was just how it should be . . .

Duncan's patient was taken away to Intensive Care and he left the theatre to relax over coffee and shop talk with his colleagues while Jennet conscientiously completed her usual tasks before handing over responsibility for Theatre Three to another sister. On her way to change, she passed the surgeons' sitting-room and saw the glint of Duncan's chestnut hair as he stood with broad back to the open door, talking to Ben Drummond and Tim Gowan, his powerful frame charged with seemingly inexhaustible energy in spite of the long hours he had spent in the operating theatre.

Her heart moved painfully in her breast. Had she really threaded her fingers through those thick, springy curls and held that handsome head to her naked breast and revelled in the heat of a desire that melted all her resistance to his seeking mouth and enfolding arms and urgent body? Had she really given virginity as well as heart to a man she had recognised at first glance as a danger?

What had happened to the sensible Sister Carter with her cautious heart and level head? Had the magic of the Greek islands cast a spell on her and sent her home from holiday in the right frame of mind to be caught up in a web of enchantment spun by a sensual surgeon? Or had it always been her destiny to love the man who had come to work at the Fitz as her father's new registrar in her brief absence on holiday?

On a sigh that was almost a sob, Jennet hurried on to the changing-room. A quick shower, a brush through her bright hair, the hasty donning of a floral silk skirt and shirt and she was ready to meet Jeff in the Main Hall. They were going to the London Collegiate where she would relieve the vigilant Verity for an hour while Jeff took her for a drink and a sandwich at a nearby pub.

He was being a tower of strength, Jennet thought gratefully, making her way towards the outer door of the unit. It was strange that she had found it so impossible to love the kindly, good-natured American who gave so much and asked so little in return. Once she had believed that she was close to it but now, deeply, throbbingly, despairingly in love with Duncan, she had learnt for herself that, while fascination might be akin to loving, it had none of the power and glory and passion of an everlasting commitment.

'Jennet! Just a moment!'

The peremptory summons echoed along the wide corridor. Struck by the unexpected use of her first name in such clinical surroundings, she turned to face the registrar, tall and impressive in theatre greens, so attractive that he cast every other man into shadow.

As he approached, one hand clenched fiercely over the bag that swung from her shoulder. The other curled itself into a tight fist in the pocket of her short, fashionable jacket. It was the only way to prevent them from stretching out to him in mute appeal. She loved him, austere and arrogant though he seemed as he strode towards her.

Just as he reached her, the doors were swung back by a gaggle of junior nurses, just arriving for duty, laughing and talking but sobering instantly at the sight of the theatre sister and surgeon.

Duncan waited, grim-faced and silent, for the girls to pass by. Then he threw open the door of a small room that was used to store empty gas cylinders and unwanted equipment and a number of theatre trolleys.

'Come in here!' he commanded. As Jennet hesitated with a doubtful look in her amber eyes, he caught her shoulder and propelled her firmly into the room. 'I want to talk to you,' he said impatiently, pained by her obvious distrust and reluctance. Tormented though he was by the need to hold her and quieten the persistent hunger for the sweetness of her lips, the softness of her breasts and the fragrance of her hair and skin teasing his senses as he crushed her close, it was a delight that must be postponed.

Jennet shrugged off the hand that sent shudders of electric desire hurtling through her slight frame. 'Can't it wait? Jeff——'

Duncan's mouth took on the grim lines that threw a disconcerting harshness over his handsome features. He might have known that making herself look beautiful for the man he regarded as a rival was the reason why she had taken so long to emerge from the changing-room, he thought savagely. But he conquered the thrust of jealous anger. 'Jeff isn't important right now,' he said brusquely, casting the man into a limbo where he might remain if fortune smiled. 'I've just been talking to Patrick Tregarron. He left a message for me to call him.'

Jennet's face blanched at the mention of the cardiologist. 'Please don't beat about the bush.' Her tone was taut.

'I'm telling it as quickly as I can, dammit!' His grey eyes softened as she flinched from the harshness of his tone. 'Sorry. I've been on edge, waiting for you. I thought you'd taken root in that damned changing-room. Patrick is very concerned about Paul. As you know, his heart was badly damaged by that succession of arrests. He's a very sick man . . .'

'Don't wrap it up, Duncan. He's going to die, isn't he?' She held her voice steady in spite of a sick dismay.

'Not if we can help it! Listen to me, woman!' He put his strong hands on her shoulders and gave her a little, impatient shake. 'I'm trying to tell you that Patrick is talking about a transplant——'

'A transplant!' The echo broke from Jennet in mingled surprise and hope. It was the last thing that she had expected, having prepared herself for the shock of bad news.

'Patrick has a cystic fibrosis patient who has been at the top of the waiting list for a heart–lung swap for some days. A donor has just become available and Patrick means to operate right away. The boy's heart is in good shape but it's proved to be more successful in such cases to replace both heart and lungs——'

'Yes, yes! I know all that!' Jennet reminded him with understandable impatience. 'Will the heart do for Paul? Can he stand major surgery?'

'It isn't a guaranteed chance of survival by any

means, but it's better than the one he's got at present,' Duncan told her bluntly.

'I see . . .' Jennet fought a rush of tears. She wasn't weak, like Verity. She wouldn't go to pieces just so that she could know the comfort and the magic of Duncan's arms about her once more. Much as she needed him, she had no claim on his concern—or his love, she reminded herself bleakly. 'Who will operate on Paul? There mustn't be any delay in transplanting the heart from one patient to another, obviously.'

'Patrick suggests that I should operate on Paul while he effects the heart-lung swap on the boy. He seems to think that I'm the right man for the job, and naturally I'd be glad to do it. What do you think, Jennet? Patrick is waiting for me to call him back as soon as I've talked to you.'

'I think it's a wonderful idea,' Jennet said without hesitation. Duncan was a brilliant surgeon who had learnt his craft at her father's side. Who better to give Paul a new heart now? Duncan had the necessary expertise and experience as well as the instinctive skill for the delicate procedure. 'What does Verity say?'

'I gather that she hasn't been consulted. You're the next of kin,' Duncan said gently.

She swallowed. She supposed that she *was*, in the circumstances, but the quiet words brought home to her the fact that Paul's condition must be critical if he was unable to sign the necessary consent form for transplant surgery.

'Call Patrick and tell him *yes*! Of course I'm in favour! I know Paul will be fine in your hands! Tell him that I'm on my way,' she said urgently, a little breathlessly.

'We'll go together . . .' Duncan bent his head to brush her quivering mouth with the lightest of kisses, a promise of more to come when the moment was more conducive to talking about the future he hoped to spend with her, an assurance that she could trust him to do everything in his power to restore her father to full and normal life, a token of the love that she had inspired and that threatened to consume him completely.

His kiss was so light, so impersonal and so fleeting that Jennet thought she recognised it for just what it was, a gesture of compassion, a promise that he would do his best for Paul and a token of the friendship that was all he could offer although she had given him her heart.

She stepped back, drawing on all the reserves of her pride. 'Jeff's waiting for me in Main Hall,' she said brightly. 'He'll take me to the hospital, Duncan. I'll see you there . . .' Thank heaven that she still had her pride—and that she could turn to Jeff to support it, she thought with a heart brimming with hurt and humiliation.

Duncan stiffened. 'Right you are,' he returned carelessly as if her retreat from him, her cool tone and her obvious desire for the American's company at this most anxious time weren't the ultimate death-blows to hope . . .

CHAPTER THIRTEEN

JEFF hurried to meet her as she appeared in the Main Hall of the hospital. 'Honey, what's wrong?' he asked in warm concern. It was unlike Jennet to have no welcoming smile for him, to glance at him with almost absent indifference, and he felt a spasm of alarm. It had been no part of his plans to fall in love with the English nurse whose friendship he had fostered to camouflage the real purpose of his trip to England. But it had happened. As a result, he lived each day with the anxiety that she would discover certain things about him to his discredit. 'Is it your father? Is he worse?'

Jennet dragged her thoughts from the brief encounter with the registrar. Dwelling on the hurt and hopelessness of loving him did no good, she told herself sensibly. She linked her hand in Jeff's arm as they turned towards the exit, grateful for his unfailing support and sympathy. 'He isn't *well*,' she admitted as if anxiety about Paul was the only thing on her mind. 'Patrick Tregarron says he needs a new heart. A transplant is being carried out this evening.'

'Then you'll want to get to the hospital as soon as possible,' Jeff said promptly and with the warm understanding that endeared him to her. 'I've a cab waiting . . .'

'You and your cabs,' she teased him, managing a smile for the extravagant habit that had become a joke between them. 'But do you mind if we take my car this time, Jeff? Transplant surgery takes hours, and then there's the business of waiting for news, and I can't expect you to sit with me and Verity through a night-long vigil. I've already taken too much advantage of your good nature, as it is.' She hugged his arm. 'I'll need my car to transport Verity back to the flat in the early hours of the morning.'

Jeff hesitated. Cabs were anonymous while private cars were easily traced and followed, and it went against all the precepts of his training to fall in with her suggestion. Also, private cars were more likely than cabs to be involved in some minor traffic incident, and it was vital that he shouldn't attract the interest of any police or other official while he was in England on this particular trip. But perhaps he could afford to take a chance, just for once . . .

'Sure, honey. That seems sensible,' he agreed. 'I have to leave you at the hospital, anyway. I don't know if I told you that I'm meeting a guy at Heathrow who's arriving at eleven on a flight from New York?' He had found that it allayed suspicion to tell people so much and no more of his movements.

He *hadn't* told Jennet. But she was already used to last-minute changes of plan where Jeff was concerned. He always seemed to be dashing off to meet or contact someone at odd hours of the day or night with very little explanation. In fact, most of his business dealings seemed to take place at night, but perhaps that involved telephone calls to colleagues in Washington, where time zoning set the clocks behind English time. In any case, it never occurred to Jennet to question him. She had no reason to doubt or distrust him, and she was too grateful for his loving support to mind his erratic behaviour.

On their way to the London Collegiate, she told Jeff something about the procedure involved in the transplant of hearts and other organs. As a layman, he was both interested and admiring. Jennet made light of the many problems that could arise and the risks that were involved in such procedures. After all, there was no point in alarming herself, she thought wryly.

As a theatre sister, she knew too well that heart transplants were not always the success stories depicted by the media. As Paul's daughter, she knew that he would need all her prayers to get him through the ordeal of long and complicated surgery. As a woman in love, she would be anxiously supporting Duncan's skilled attempt to ensure a better and brighter future for her father, in spirit if not in the flesh, for, much as she would have liked to assist him, she knew he wouldn't ask it and she was in no position to put herself forward at a hospital where she wasn't employed.

With the image of Duncan in his theatre greens flickering in her mind's eye, Jennet's concentration lapsed for a moment and she failed to see the sports car that hurtled out of a side turning to cross the path of the Sierra. Then, instinctively, she stood on the brake.

She shouted a warning, too, but Jeff had neglected to check that his seatbelt was securely buckled, and he was thrown forward by the jolt of the emergency stop, hitting his head sharply on the windscreen. Knocked out, he slumped with blood flowing from his nose and a cut above his eye.

Better restrained, Jennet's ribs were still bruised by the sudden impact with the steering wheel and her knee collided angrily with the dashboard. But she scarcely noticed her own bumps and bruises in her concern for the unconscious man at her side. The sports car was rapidly receding from the scene, its driver either unaware or unconcerned that his bad driving had caused her to brake so abruptly.

The driver of a following car had been sufficiently distanced from the Sierra to take evasive action as it slewed across the road on a squeal of brakes. Pulling up a few yards ahead of the halted car, he hurried back to help, a swift glance as he overtook having observed the shock on Jennet's face and the slumped figure of her passenger.

He threw open the car door, pale with concern, grey eyes dark with fury. 'That stupid bastard ought to be shot!' he raged. 'The maniac might have killed you! Are you all right, my darling?'

Struggling to hold Jeff upright and trying to stanch the blood from his nose and eyebrow, she was too preoccupied and too anxious to notice the betraying warmth and tenderness of the endearment. 'Oh, Duncan!' she breathed gratefully, thankful that he had such a talent for turning up when he was most needed. It was opportune that he had been going to the hospital by the same route at the same time although she had been unaware of the following car. 'Am I glad to see *you*! I'm fine. It's Jeff! He hit his head on the windscreen when I braked and I think he's concussed . . .'

'Then we'd better get him to Casualty and have him checked out as soon as possible. We're only a few minutes away from the hospital, fortunately. Get in the back and I'll drive . . .'

Duncan took charge with the briskness that had led to accusations of arrogance but Jennet didn't mind. She was glad to hand over the responsibility for getting Jeff to a hospital to someone so confident and so capable. In fact, she would dearly love to put herself into those strong, sure hands and know herself safe for the rest of her life, she thought wistfully as she obediently clambered from the driving seat.

She winced as she put her weight on her bruised knee, and Duncan instantly caught her shoulder, scanning her face.

'Are you sure that you're OK?'

'I banged my knee, that's all,' she said dismissively.

'You seem a bit shaken.'

'I'm worried about Jeff.' On top of everything else, she might have added.

'Yes. Of course you are.' Duncan's hand fell at the reminder that her concern, her heart and her future were all caught up with the American, except where her father was concerned. Leaning into the car to unlock the rear door for her, he heard a slight groan from his unexpected patient. Instantly, he was doctor rather than despairing lover as training took over from emotion. Sliding into the driving seat, he felt for the man's pulse and lifted an eyelid to check for dilation of the pupils. Some of Jeff's blood stained the cuff of his shirt. 'He's coming round,' he reassured Jennet as she got into the car. 'But we won't waste any time in getting him to hospital for X-rays . . .'

By the time the car drew up outside the accident and emergency department of the hospital that had become much too familiar to Jennet, Jeff was conscious but dazed and sick and shaken, complaining of a headache and gingerly fingering a possibly broken nose. Jennet sped into the building and was back in a matter of moments with a casualty officer and porters with a stretcher trolley. Jeff was carefully helped from the car and wheeled into the hospital for examination.

'You'd better have that knee looked at, too,' Duncan commanded as he followed Jennet into the reception area.

'It's only bruised,' she demurred.

'Never mind. It's obviously painful.'

'Yes, Doctor.'

He caught a glimpse of her lovely smile as she mocked him with the demure words. He looked down at her as they paused beside the desk, fighting the need to sweep her into his arms and hold her against his heart. 'I don't like leaving you at this point but I must, I'm afraid. Everything's waiting on my arrival in Theatres and I still have to change into greens and scrub up . . .' As Paul was being treated as a private patient, there was no problem about offering his services as a cardiac surgeon in a different hospital from the one that had him under contract.

'Of course you must go! Don't worry about me, Duncan.' Jennet put a hand on his arm, giving in to the desperate need for brief physical contact with the man who meant so much to her. She smiled up at him, doing her best to keep the light of love from shining out of her eyes. 'I know Paul will be fine. You'll pull him through,' she said trustingly, her voice wobbling just a little. 'I just wish that I could be at your side, assisting.'

'I wouldn't want you around,' he told her bluntly, knowing that she would be a distraction and an anxiety. She was a highly trained hospital sister, skilled and experienced in theatre work, and he knew that she could be trusted to keep her head in most circumstances, but he had no wish for her presence in the theatre while he carried out life-saving surgery on her father. For one thing, it was unethical. For another, it would be too traumatic for Jennet and too difficult for him to be detached about his work when it was a case of such vital importance to the woman he loved with all his heart. 'Do me a favour and keep well away until it's all over, Jennet. Your place is with Verity. She'll need you more than ever tonight.'

Resentment rose in Jennet's breast at the reminder that his concern was first and foremost for her friend. 'Right now, my place is with Jeff,' she said sharply, just as if she were committed by love rather than a feeling of guilt. 'I must stay with him until we get the results of the X-rays and know if he'll be admitted or sent home. There's no problem if he's kept overnight for observation but if he isn't, then I must see that he gets back to his hotel, at least. I just hope he'll trust me to drive him! In any case, I can't desert him, can I?' She walked away, seething with hurt and anger, and joined Jeff in the cubicle where he waited to be taken to the X-ray department after a brief examination by the casualty officer.

She couldn't have put it more plainly, Duncan thought heavily, as he made his way to Theatres where adjoining operating-rooms were being got ready for dual transplant surgery. Her place was with the American, she felt. Not only that night but for always, no doubt—and even anxiety for her father couldn't tear her from the man's side until she was reassured about the effect of that blow on the head. Well, that was very natural if she loved the man. There was nothing that Jennet could do for Paul for the next few hours, and perhaps it was just as well that she had something else to think about, he decided generously.

It was no use hoping that she might be thinking and feeling for him during the long hours ahead of him . . .

Jeff clutched at Jennet's hand as she sat down beside the couch with a reassuring smile. 'Honey, I have to talk to you!' he said urgently.

'Yes, but not now,' she soothed, knowing the importance of keeping him calm and quiet. 'Relax and try not to talk, Jeff. You've had a nasty knock on the head. I can't tell you how sorry I am——'

'It wasn't your fault.'

'It *was*, in a way, I should have seen that wretched car! Luckily, I didn't hit it—and if you'd been wearing the seatbelt . . .' She broke off, contrite. Reproaching him only rubbed salt in his wounds, after all. 'What did the doctor say about your nose?'

'He doesn't think it's broken. Just bruised. I'll have a black eye tomorrow, though.' He managed a wry grin. 'I guess I've got to wait for three X-rays but I hope it won't take too long.'

'You may have to stay in hospital for the night, Jeff,' she warned him.

'Hell, honey! I can't do that!' He struggled to sit up, looking alarmed. 'I've got to meet Jasper at the airport tonight! It's important!'

'That's obviously out of the question,' Jennet said firmly. 'But don't worry, Jeff. I'll see to it that a message is waiting for your friend when he arrives at Heathrow. I'm sure he'll understand . . .'

'You don't understand, Jennet! A message just won't do! He's only making a stopover before he flies on to Johannesburg and I've an important package that must get to him before he leaves England.' He reached for the jacket slung across the back of her chair and drew a thick envelope from the inner pocket. 'God, I feel lousy,' he complained, lying back against the pillow that supported his aching head. 'Honey, I can't go to the airport. I feel too bad. But *you* can! Will you do that for me? Will you see that this envelope reaches Jasper Irving on Pan Am Flight 602 from New York—give it to him yourself, I mean? Don't give it over to anyone else, for God's sake. It's important, Jennet. Do you understand?' He put a hand to his head and gave a groan.

Jennet was torn. She needed to be on hand in case anything happened to Paul—her mind veered from the idea—and at the same time she felt responsible for what had happened to Jeff. She knew that she ought to do as he asked if it were really so important. The last thing she wanted to do was drive to Heathrow in the late evening and accost a stranger on the concourse.

'Jasper's leaving England tonight and he needs what's in this package,' Jeff insisted urgently. 'I'm relying on you, honey. Don't let me down! If this deal goes through we'll celebrate by getting married and to hell with my old man's approval.'

Jennet's smile was uncertain as she reluctantly took the package that he thrust at her. 'All right. I'll take it. But your appointment isn't until eleven, is it? You might feel much better by then and I don't mind driving you . . .'

'It's obvious that I won't be fit enough for anything tonight,' he snapped with uncharacteristic but understandable impatience. 'Damn it, Jennet! I had a cab waiting!'

'Yes, I know,' she agreed guiltily, thinking that for once Jeff's preference for travelling by taxi had been justified. 'I'm really sorry . . .' There seemed to be little else she could say.

'OK, OK. I'm not blaming you,' he said wearily, closing his eyes to shield them from the lights that made his headache worse. 'And there's no real harm done as long as you get that package to Jasper.'

'I will. I promise,' Jennet reassured him, and he described how to recognise Jasper Irving. Then she had to reach for a bowl as he changed colour, and hold his head as he vomited. He had all the symptoms of concussion and she hoped that X-rays wouldn't show signs of more serious injury. Anxious as she was to know what was happening in Theatres, she felt that she ought to stay with Jeff for the time being.

Fortunately, the X-ray results were reassuring, but Jeff was admitted for observation and Jennet saw him settled on the ward before she finally felt free to leave him to sleep off the effects of the accident.

'Duncan told me what happened,' Verity said in greeting as Jennet walked into the waiting-room. 'Are you all right? No delayed shock or anything?'

'Just a tremendous relief that Jeff isn't much hurt,' Jennet sighed. 'He was out for a few minutes so he's been kept in for the night, but it seems to be only a minor concussion, thank heavens. How are you? What's happening?' She was thankful that Verity seemed so calm. She had expected her to be distraught and weeping.

'It's too soon for progress reports but I gather that both Paul and the boy are undergoing preliminary surgery at the moment. Duncan is so optimistic that I'm sure everything will be all right. It's just a matter of waiting.'

Her tone was so impersonal that she might have been discussing one of her own patients rather than the man she loved and hoped to marry. Her hands lay on the arms of her chair, so ominously still rather than relaxed that Jennet hoped that her friend's careful composure wouldn't crack at the worst possible moment.

Verity was obviously pinning her hopes on Duncan's expertise and experience. Well, so was she, Jennet reminded herself, desperately trying not to mind that he must have snatched a few extra minutes to see Verity in spite of the fact that his presence was so urgently required in Theatres. Very natural behaviour for a man in love, surely—and the sooner she accepted the plain truth that there was no future for her with the clever and caring Duncan Blair, the better for her peace of mind, Jennet told herself sternly.

Hoping to divert Verity from the thought of what was happening to Paul, she told her about Jeff's business appointment and her own proposed trip to Heathrow in his place.

'It seems the least I can do, in the circumstances,' she finished wryly. 'I hope not to be too long. Shall I drive you back to the flat first so that you can have a meal and a shower and get some rest? I'll come back for you later, of course. It's going to be hours before there's any real news, you know.'

'I'll come with you,' Verity said instantly. 'It will give us both something to do, and I'm sure you can't want to drive out to the airport on your own.'

'If you like.' Jennet was surprised but grateful for the offer of company. 'If you're sure that you want to come . . .'

'Oh, yes. I love airports.'

Jennet could think of better places. But a hospital waiting-room at a time like this wasn't one of them, she conceded.

Both girls made a conscious effort to be cheerful and confident about the outcome of Paul's operation as they drove to Heathrow. They talked about a number of things, carefully avoiding the subject of hospitals and surgeons—and particularly hearts! They stopped for a meal and arrived at the airport about half an hour before the flight from New York was due. No delays were announced. The two girls found a seat near the Customs exit and settled down to wait, watching the to and fro of people who were flying in and out of the country or waiting to meet friends and relatives.

It was only a few weeks since Jennet had herself flown in on her way home from holiday with head and heart full of a romantic conquest in Greece. Much to her surprise, Jeff had remained on the scene, but the dream of him had been knocked sideways by the introduction of a very different man into her life. Jeff had touched her heart. Duncan had captured it completely.

The minutes ticked away and the girls began to feel restive, anxious to get back to the hospital for news. Then a tall, bearded and obviously travel-weary passenger emerged, and stood looking about him, obviously expecting to meet someone. Jennet recalled Jeff's description of his friend. Getting to her feet, she slowly walked towards Jasper Irving, a hand tugging at the zip of her shoulder bag, wondering if she ought to ask for some identification before handing over an apparently important package to a stranger. He seemed wary, ill at ease, turning away to scan the concourse, no doubt wondering why Jeff had failed to turn up as expected.

Two men brushed past Jennet. One laid a detaining hand on Jasper Irving's arm. Courteously, discreetly but firmly, they showed official identity cards and requested him to accompany them to Security. With a resigned shrug of his shoulders that belied the angry glitter in his eyes, he walked off with them.

Backing away, Jennet hastily returned to Verity and sat down, shocked and bewildered. 'They were *police*!' she said, horrified.

'Or Customs men. It looks as if your Jasper Irving has been a naughty boy,' Verity said drily. 'You might have been caught up in something very nasty if you'd handed over that package. What's in it, anyway? Did Jeff tell you?'

'Business papers, I think,' Jennet said doubtfully, gingerly fingering the envelope concealed in her bag. 'I don't know . . .'

'It could be diamonds. Or drugs. Or top secret documents. Let's have a look,' Verity suggested sensibly.

Jennet shook her head. 'I'm not opening it. Whatever it contains. I'll just give it back to Jeff and explain what happened.'

'And hope *he* can explain why his friend should be arrested as soon as he showed, I suppose? If he hasn't been arrested, too! You really don't know very much about him, do you, Jennet? Lord knows what he's mixed up in—and Duncan has never trusted him.' Verity spoke as if Duncan's distrust should have been sufficient to warn Jennet against the American. 'You ought to take that package to the police.'

'And implicate Jeff! I can't do that!'

'He was prepared to implicate you! Not very lover-like behaviour, is it?' Verity said scathingly.

Jennet sighed. 'I wish I knew *what* to do . . .'

'Ask Duncan. He's the best person to advise you,' Verity urged with implicit faith in the surgeon's ability to provide all the answers. She yanked Jennet to her feet. 'Come on—let's get out of here! We haven't any time to waste here!'

Jennet limped after her friend, conscious of her bruised knee and half expecting to find a posse of policemen waiting for them outside the terminal . . .

CHAPTER FOURTEEN

THE wards were hushed, most patients sleeping and night staff going quietly about their routines when Jennet and Verity got back to the London Collegiate. In the Theatre Unit attached to the Cardiac Unit, arc lights still blazed and the two teams of surgeons still worked tirelessly on the exchange of hearts.

A troubled Jennet rang the ward to which Jeff had been admitted and learnt, to her astonishment and dismay, that he had demanded his clothes and discharged himself soon after she left for the airport. He had signed a form absolving the hospital authorities from all responsibility if he collapsed as a result of the concussion from which he was suffering.

Instantly she telephoned the Hilton, but Jeff had checked out of the hotel even before he met her at the Fitz in the early evening.

'It seems as though he was anticipating trouble,' Verity said sagely. 'Duncan was right, Jennet. He *isn't* just an ordinary businessman over here to do a deal—and he's been stringing you along for reasons of his own. Now, you *must* open that envelope.'

Jennet took it reluctantly from her bag. 'I suppose so . . .'

It was well sealed. Her fumbling fingers took so long to prise it apart that the impatient Verity seized it from her. 'It's a passport!'

Colour drained from Jennet's cheeks. 'And a wallet . . .' A leather notecase with stamped gold initials that was too familiar for comfort.

Verity had no compunction about opening it. 'Money . . . American dollars, some sterling—and a pack of credit cards.'

Jennet gingerly picked up the passport with the American eagle on the cover. 'It's Jeff's own passport,' she discovered, heart sinking. 'I don't understand this at all, Verity.'

Verity looked over her shoulder. 'But that isn't Jeff.' She indicated the identifying photograph. 'That's the man we saw at the airport, complete with beard. No wonder he needed these things so urgently if he meant to fly out of the country almost immediately. It's a change of identity, Jennet! And if Jeff hadn't hit his head in your car it might well have come off!' Excitement tinged her tone.

'But Jeff needs his passport. He can't leave the country without it.'

'I expect he's got another one—in a different name,' Verity said drily. 'And I bet it isn't Jasper Irving!' She took the wallet from Jennet's lap and drew out more of its contents, including a letter that enclosed photographs of a slim brunette and three small children. 'Look at this, Jennet! "Darling Jeff . . ."' she quoted, and riffled hastily through the few pages to the signature. '"The kids send their love and we all miss you, Daddy. Come home soon. Your loving Beth . . ." Oh, Jennet, he's really taken you for a ride! He probably isn't Jefferson B. Lloyd at all! But I bet he *does* have a wife and kids tucked away in the States!'

Jennet gathered up the incriminating effects and thrust them back into the envelope, her hands shaking, feeling sick that she had been so deceived and misled into helping a stranger met on holiday in something that was obviously illegal and might well be dangerous. And she had almost fallen in love with him! How much worse she would be feeling now if she had! And supposing she *had* gone to bed with a man who might be a criminal or a spy or even a terrorist!

Somehow, she knew instinctively that Jeff *was* married, even if that photograph was not of his wife and children but merely another brick in a wall of deceit that had been intended to block detection by the police, if not for himself but for that other man.

He had been tender and loving, but never as persistent or as persuasive as a man in love might be expected to be, and there had been moments when he had hesitated to take advantage of her weakness when she clung to him beneath the stars on a deserted beach or a quiet terrace on that beautiful Greek island. Perhaps love and loyalty to another woman had stayed his desire and kept him faithful to a wife who waited for him to return from a 'business' trip. She must be grateful for that much, at least, Jennet told herself devoutly. But she certainly hoped that she would never see him again. He had used her affection and her friendship as well as her respectable status as a hospital sister to cover up some nefarious activity while he was in England, perhaps hoping to put police or government agents off his scent, and, as Verity urged, she must hand over the package and its suspicious contents to some official as soon as possible.

Jeff had felt no compunction about involving her

and exposing her to possible arrest and a charge of complicity or worse. He might have ruined her career and maybe her whole life, and she couldn't forgive him for that. Fortunately, she owed him nothing and he could be easily forgotten, she told herself thankfully.

Verity put a comforting hand on her arm. 'I'm so sorry,' she said gently, knowing how her friend must feel. 'It's awful for you . . .'

Jennet braced her slim shoulders. 'I'm furious,' she said. 'Absolutely livid!' Amber eyes sparkled with anger as she leapt to her feet and began to pace the small area of waiting-room attached to the Cardiac Unit. 'He really made a fool of me! I *trusted* him, Verity. I believed every word he said! That's the last time *I* shall look twice at a man I meet on holiday!' she added bitterly.

'It could happen to anyone,' Verity soothed. 'I liked him, too.'

'Oh, he's a smoothie. Everyone liked him. Everyone but Duncan.' Jennet made a face. 'The hard part will be admitting that Duncan was right about him,' she said wryly. 'He warned me weeks ago that Jeff was trouble and I just wouldn't listen.'

'What woman listens to anything but her heart when she's in love?' Verity sympathised. She knew, and understood. She had been warned, too. But she had no regrets about loving a man twice her age and at present undergoing vital heart surgery. Paul was going to pull through, and she would nurse him back to health and the resumption of his brilliant career and they would spend many happy years together, she told herself confidently.

'I'm not in love with Jeff, I'm glad to say!' Jennet disillusioned her friend in a firm tone. 'What on earth gives you that idea?'

'The kind of behaviour that has given Duncan exactly the same idea,' Verity retorted drily. 'You are an idiot, Jennet! If you don't care tuppence for the man, why allow Duncan to think that you do? You're putting him through hell!'

Jennet stared. '*Duncan!*'

'We're talking about Duncan, aren't we? Of course *Duncan*! I can't believe that you don't know how he feels about you.'

'I know how he feels about *you*,' Jennet said heavily.

Verity laughed the suggestion to scorn. 'This is turning into a comedy of errors! You've been making each other miserable and don't even know it! Duncan's a friend—a good friend to Paul *and* me. That's all. He's eating his heart out over *you*.'

'Well, he has a funny way of showing it,' Jennet denied stubbornly, considering it much too dangerous to allow herself to hope even for a moment that the assurance might be true. But if only it *were* . . .

Verity shrugged and fell silent. She had done her best for Duncan. Now it was up to him to convince Jennet that he cared for her—and a wistful gleam in those amber eyes hinted that she was ready to meet him more than half-way, she thought with quiet satisfaction.

It was a long night of waiting for news, broken only by cups of tea and sympathetic noises from the night staff, who did their best to be reassuring about the drama being enacted in the operating theatres at the end of the corridor. Neither Jennet nor Verity pointed out that they probably knew more than the nurses about the difficulties of microsurgery in such procedures.

Tired and anxious, they found it impossible to sleep and, as tension mounted, difficult to talk about anything but the one thing uppermost in both their minds. They supported each other through the hours, bonded by their mutual concern for Paul and the longing to be playing some part in the dual exchange of hearts. As qualified doctor and experienced theatre sister, they weren't helped by knowing so much about cardiac surgery and its potential dangers.

Information finally began to filter through in the early hours of the morning. Paul's donor had come safely through the surgery that had given him new heart and lungs and he had been taken to Intensive Care.

There were one or two problems in Paul's case, the two girls were told with a casual ambiguity that did nothing for their peace of mind. Both knew that the light words possibly cloaked the fact that Paul had arrested on the operating-table or that the new heart had proved to be totally unsuitable.

Verity was surprisingly calm as they waited for further news. Jennet envied her supreme confidence in the outcome. For her part, she was besieged by a nagging doubt.

Haunted by so much evidence in so many ways that Duncan really loved Verity and not herself, she wondered if he could be totally dedicated to saving the life of a man who must seem to be an obstacle to his happiness. He might be a clever and caring surgeon, but if he was also a man in love then surely there was the risk of a conflict of aims? Unconscious, perhaps, but maybe affecting his work to a dangerous degree, none the less.

Poor Jennet was cold and sick with anxiety for her father and even more desperately anxious not to be faced with the suspicion that the man she loved had feet of clay. Her love for Duncan was a mix of longing, of admiration for his brilliance, of respect for his integrity. But if Paul died—and heart surgery always carried that risk—then she might always wonder if Duncan had tried hard enough to ensure that he lived.

The experience with Jeff had undermined her faith in her own judgement where men were concerned, she admitted ruefully. Having been so mistaken in one man, had she been equally wrong to trust another not only with her body in a moment of madness but also with her heart? Since the night that had been such a memorable one, Duncan had not said a single word to her that she could store away for comfort at moments like these, she thought unhappily. She loved him so much. Surely, if he loved her, he would have sensed her aching need of him and responded to it. With a word, a smile, a reassuring touch, if nothing more . . .

Both Jennet and Verity leapt to their feet as Duncan appeared in the doorway, powerful shoulders in sweat-darkened greens filling the frame. His chestnut hair was damp and tousled where he had pulled off his cap on leaving the operating theatre. He looked pale and weary, and too tense for immediate speech. He was the bearer of tidings, good or bad, and at first there was no indication of which in the steady gaze of deep-set grey eyes.

It was only seconds before he spoke. It seemed like an eternity to the anxious girls. Jennet swallowed, throat dry and constricting with anxiety.

Conscious of Verity's taut figure, she braced herself
to cope if her friend collapsed on receipt of bad
news. Her own heart thudded with dread, touched
by the cold fingers of fear, but she knew that she
could face the worst with the strength that Duncan
had already recognised and admired.

'He's OK. He'll do,' Duncan said quietly and
held out his arms to both girls, smiling. With a little
sob, Verity cast herself on his breast and clung.
Jennet allowed herself to clutch at his strong hand,
the hand that had spent so many hours working
so skilfully to give her father a new chance of life,
with relief and gratitude in the shine of her amber
eyes. He took her hand to his lips and kissed it,
warm tenderness in his continuing smile.

Verity pulled away. 'Can I see him?'

'For two seconds and no more. And one at a
time,' he warned.

Verity hesitated, glancing at Jennet, and hung
back. Jennet gave her a little push, understanding.
'Go on . . .' Different kinds of loving had different
claims. She was only Paul's daughter. Verity was
his love, and her need to see Paul took precedence
over her own.

As Verity's hurrying footsteps rang out along the
corridor, Jennet smiled shyly at Duncan. 'I don't
know how to thank you . . .'

'There's only one way that will satisfy me.'
Duncan drew her into his arms and looked deep
into the wondering amber eyes. Sometimes a man
had to reach out for what he wanted with a
confidence that it wouldn't be denied instead of
wondering and waiting and worrying that she was
destined for another man. Jennet belonged to
him—whether she knew it or not! 'I'm a surgeon,

Jennet. I do my best for all my patients. But I gave a little more of myself tonight.' He laid his tired head against her soft curls. 'Do you know why, my love?'

Jennet caught her breath. The fold of his strong arms, the glow in the grey eyes and the warmth of wanting that emanated from him told her, but she wanted to hear it from his lips. 'Tell me . . .' she breathed.

'Because Paul's my very good friend.'

'*Oh* . .' Disappointed, disbelieving, she drew away, tilting her head to look up at him with reproachful eyes.

'And because, with any luck, he'll soon be my father-in-law,' Duncan went on, arms tightening securely about the woman he loved. 'Are you grateful enough to marry me, do you think? Because it's the one thing I want more than anything else in the world, my darling.'

Jennet nestled happily into his arms. 'You drive a hard bargain, Duncan Blair,' she murmured in mock protest, smiling up at him.

'It isn't a bargain, Sister Carter. I'm offering a fair exchange, surely. Your heart for mine,' he said softly and kissed her.

The power of love was in his kiss, and sweet yielding of heart and body and soul into his keeping in her eager response.

Fair exchange, indeed, Jennet decided thankfully. An exchange of loving hearts . . .

ROMANCING THE PHONE

Win the romantic holiday of a lifetime for two at the exclusive Couples Hotel in Ocho Rios on Jamaica's north coast with the Mills & Boon and British Telecom's novel competition, 'Romancing the Phone'.

This exciting competition looks at the importance the telephone call plays in romance. All you have to do is write a story or extract about a romance involving the phone which lasts approximately two minutes when read aloud.

The winner will not only receive the holiday in Jamaica, but the entry will also be heard by millions of people when it is included in a selection of extracts from a short list of entries on British Telecom's 'Romance Line'. Regional winners and runners up will receive British Telecom telephones, answer machines and Mills & Boon books.

For an entry leaflet and further details all you have to do is call 01 400 5359, or write to 'Romancing the Phone', 22 Endell Street, London WC2H 9AD.

You may be mailed with other offers as a result of this application.

COUPLES.

DESPERADO – Helen Conrad   £2.75

In this fast-paced and compelling novel, jewel thief and
embezzler, Michael Drayton, has a five thousand dollar
price on his head. With Jessie MacAllister after the
reward and hot on his trail, the Desperado turns on his
devasting charm, leaving her with one key dilemma...
how to turn him in!

ONCE AND FOR ALWAYS
Stella Cameron   £2.99

The magic and beauty of Wales and the picturesque
fishing village, Tenby, form the backdrop to Stella
Cameron's latest poignant novel. Caitlin McBride's past
reads like a fairytale, and returning to Tenby seems to
offer the only escape from a dead marriage and hellish
family life. But would the spell still exist – and would
she find the love she had once left behind?

Published: DECEMBER 1989

W**O**RLDWIDE

Available from Boots, Martins,
John Menzies, W.H. Smith, Woolworths
and other paperback stockists.

A SPARKLING COLLECTION FOR CHRISTMAS FROM

TEMPTATION

This special Temptation Christmas pack has 4 novels all based on a single theme – the Montclair Emeralds. Enjoy and discover the exciting mystique and the secrets of these magnificent gems.

The pack features four of our most popular authors.

Fulfilment	–	Barbara Delinsky
Trust	–	Rita Clay Estrada
Joy	–	Jayne Ann Krentz
Impulse	–	Vicki Lewis Thompson

PLUS, with each pack you have a chance to enter the fabulous Temptation Emeralds competition.

Available from Boots, Martins, John Menzies, WH Smith, Woolworths and other paperback stockists.

Pub. Date
3rd November 1989

Mills & Boon

Price £5